LIVE FAE OR DIE TRYING

THE PARANORMAL PI FILES - BOOK ONE

JENNA WOLFHART

This book was produced in the UK using British English, and the setting is London. Some spelling and word usage may differ from US English.

~

Live Fae or Die Trying

Book One in The Paranormal PI Files

Cover Design by Covers by Juan

Copyright © 2019 by Jenna Wolfhart

All rights reserved.

No part of this book may be reproduced in any form or by any electronic or mechanical means, including information storage and retrieval systems, without written permission from the author, except for the use of brief quotations in a book review.

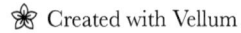

❦ Created with Vellum

ALSO BY JENNA WOLFHART

The Paranormal PI Files

Live Fae or Die Trying

Dead Fae Walking

Bad Fae Rising

The Bone Coven Chronicles

Witch's Curse

Witch's Storm

Witch's Blade

Witch's Fury

Protectors of Magic

Wings of Stone

Carved in Stone

Bound by Stone

Shadows of Stone

Order of the Fallen

Ruinous

Nebulous

Ravenous

Otherworld Academy

A Dance with Darkness

A Song of Shadows

A Touch of Starlight

Dark Fae Academy

A Cage of Moonlight

A Heart of Midnight

A Throne of Illusions (Coming Soon!)

1

I was trapped in my East London flat with two angry werewolves, and things were starting to get dicey. I'd just dropped a load of evidence a.k.a shite, and neither one of them were particularly thrilled by the info. The shifters were one breath away from transforming my living room office into a supernatural war zone.

"Let's take a step back, shall we?" Gritting my teeth, I held up my hands and stepped between them. Normally, when supes got a little rowdy, I just let them have at it. Fight intervention wasn't in my private investigator job description. Unfortunately, my landlord's long-enduring patience had officially run out three tussles ago. There were a dozen dents already smattered across my walls. If these shifters added to the collection? I was out.

And I had nowhere else to go.

I placed a palm on one werewolf's chest and winced when he responded with a deep-throated growl. His name was Lucian, and he was as grizzled as you'd expect. Despite living in London, there was a wildness about him that gave away his supernatural heritage. Long, dark hair curled around his ears, and his eyes flashed between yellow and red. He was also, incidentally, about seven feet tall.

I, on the other hand, barely hit five foot two.

"How am I supposed to calm down after what you just told me, Clark?" His eyes flashed red, and he twisted his gaze toward his friend and fellow pack member, Raoul. Well, former friend. Lucian had hired me to look into his wife's suspected infidelity. He'd been worried that a wolf from another pack had been wooing her in secret. Turned out he'd been right. Another wolf *had* been wooing her, just one from his own pack.

It was a betrayal of epic proportions, particularly for wolves. Packs were family. They were a unit. They were blood.

"Maybe if Lucian hadn't been too consumed with pack business, Olivia wouldn't have felt the need to seek out companionship elsewhere," Raoul said with a sneer, shaking his long mane of reddish hair.

Lucian growled. Raoul growled. The hair along their arms began to sprout. And I was standing smack dab in the middle of the whole thing.

I wet my lips, my heart hammering hard. If these two shifted into wolves and fought, my flat's survival wouldn't be the only thing I'd have to worry about. I might be half-fae, but I wasn't trained, and I didn't have full access to my powers.

I was Courtless, which meant I lived outside of supernatural law—and without full control of the magic that came along with the fae side of me. Sure, I could read minds—which was how I'd found out exactly what Raoul and Olivia had been up to—but my physical capabilities? Well, they were lacking, to say the least.

Of course, I was also half-shifter myself, but I had never transformed into an animal in my life. So, that wasn't particularly helpful either.

But my warnings were too late, or they were just flat-out ignored. The bodies of both shifters began to shimmer, every limb contorting into impossible shapes. Bones snapped, jaws and teeth lengthened. In less than a moment's time, two snarling, massive beasts hunkered on my hardwood floor, their nostrils flaring as they glared at each other.

This...was not ideal.

I stumbled back and ducked behind my office desk—a dilapidated thing I'd found next to the dumpster down the street. Chewing gum had been smashed underneath it. The whole thing had seriously wobbled until I'd shoved a book under one of the legs. Still, it was a desk, and it would do just fine as a hiding place.

Lucian—or Raoul, I couldn't be sure—smashed the desk sideways. I ducked low to avoid the impact. It slammed into the wall behind me, splintering into at least ten different pieces. My heart thumped, and I swallowed hard. So much for that.

The wolf now stood over me, his entire body trembling as his yellow eyes narrowed into sharp little points. I was not his enemy, but...he didn't know that. The problem with wolves? They were volatile. Their thoughts and their emotions ran wild, just like them. A lot of times, they forgot themselves, particularly if they shifted with too much emotion running through their veins.

That meant it was easy enough for them to forget themselves. So, while Raoul and Lucian knew they were angry about *something*…they might just decide that they were angry with me instead of each other.

With a shuddering breath, I pushed up from the ground, curled my hands into fists, and took slow steps back toward my bedroom door. Time for me to make a hasty escape, as much as I hated to turn tail and run. The werewolves crept in closer, their sharp eyes watching my every move like I was prey they needed to slaughter.

Just think, I said to myself, trying to see the potential pro of this particular insane situation, *if you survive this, you'll have a hell of a story for the podcast.*

I, Clark Cavanaugh, wasn't just a paranormal private investigator. In fact, that wasn't how I made my living most of the time. Supernaturals came out to the world ten years ago. While some were wealthy, like the fae, others weren't. They relied on their jobs. Jobs they promptly lost when humans found out the truth about our world. Turned out, humans weren't too keen on working with werewolves and vampires, *but* they definitely wanted to hear about their drama.

Since most supes couldn't afford my services, and since I was usually desperate for some cash, I offered to take on their cases for free in exchange for some podcasting love. I could talk about their case on the air after I solved it, bringing in loads of listeners and sponsorship deals. I earned enough to live. Barely. So, things had worked out just fine. Except for the whole fighting thing that tended to happen.

Supes, while powerful, weren't great at controlling their tempers.

Case in point: the two angry werewolves stalking toward me, their fur trembling with each impossibly-deep breath they took. Their yellowed eyes were locked on my face, and their long snouts sucked at the air, sensing and sniffing my fear.

There had to be a way to remedy this. I probed at their minds, hoping I could pick something from their thoughts that could help me calm them down, but I was immediately thrown underneath an avalanche of churning thoughts.

Taste her flesh! Chase her down! Her scent, her fear, her delicious skin.

Gritting my teeth, I closed my eyes to block it out, but it was too late. I'd opened my mind to them, and now it was hard to shut them out. My power was strong, but...sometimes, it was too strong. While it was easy to control around humans, it was much more difficult around supes, especially when they were charged with so much energy.

Bite, kill, taste!

I fell to the ground, pressing my hands over my ears and chanting nonsensical words underneath my breath. Not that it would do any good. I didn't actually hear a damn thing with my ears, only with my mind. And I'd never been taught how to get control once the thoughts began to flood through me.

Eat! Taste! Give her to me!

A single word here and there, tumbling on top of each other. The voices were so loud that I couldn't even hear myself think.

"That will be all, gentleman," a deep lyrical voice

said just as the voices snapped off. An ice cold voice. One I had heard once before. Chills swept along my skin as I glanced up from where I cowered in the corner. My eyes swept toward the open door where Balor Beimnech, the most powerful and dangerous fae prince alive, stood staring at me with a single glittering red eye. His other eye was hidden beneath a black patch, his signature apparel. No one had ever seen his second eye. Or, at least, no one had lived to tell about it. Rumor had it that it was lit with fire, and anything he looked at would burst into brutal, uncontrollable flames.

Balor, the smiter.

I wet my lips and pushed myself up from the floor, my heart hammering even harder. The shifters were beginning to transform back into their non-animal shapes, but I didn't feel a single bit better about the situation.

Balor had found me.

Like I said before, I was Courtless. That meant I had no bond, no loyalty to any fae Court or any House. It also meant that I was an outcast. Hell, an *outlaw*. I'd done my best to hide among the London streets, hoping to avoid a confrontation with the fae that ruled the supernatural world of this city. I didn't want to join a Court. There was too much about my past that I needed to keep hidden. If they found out who I was and where I'd come from...they'd want me dead.

Especially Balor Beimnech.

Unfortunately, I'd caught Balor's attention two weeks ago during an intel-gathering mission for my only friend, Ondine. He'd insisted I join his Court right then and there, but I'd evaded his capture.

By, um, kneeing him in the balls. It wasn't a move I was proud of, but it had worked.

Until now, apparently.

Shit.

He took a step into the room, his tall, muscular body radiating with power. His thick dark hair was cut through with slices of silver, and his strong jaw rippled as he took in the scene. The annoying thing about Balor was that he was so hot he made my toes curl. He also smelled intoxicating, like rich leather, smoky mist, and the deepest parts of the forest.

I had to keep myself together though. So that I could run like hell.

"Clark," he said, his voice almost a purr. "It seems you have a bloody mess on your hands."

So, he'd found out my name. That wasn't a good sign. I'd done my best to keep my head down these past two weeks, even barely sharing info on my podcast. I knew he'd be looking for me. I just hadn't expected him to find me this easily.

Of course, while I'd been hiding, I'd also been trying to snoop on him. Just a little. Ondine suspected that he was behind the recent disappearances of some female fae in his Court, and I'd sworn to her that I'd check things out. Reading his thoughts had proved impossible. His mind was a steel trap, and I couldn't get inside.

"No problem," I said in a chirpy tone. "Lucian and Raoul here were just leaving. Right, boys?"

The two wolves, now looking quite chagrined, cleared their throats and nodded, not even bothering to right the desk they'd smashed into the wall. Typical shifters.

As they passed Balor on their way out the door, they gave a slight nod of respect and deference. The supernatural community had certain tiers, depending on the strength of an individual's powers. Shifters were near the bottom, topped by sorcerers, and then vampires. Fae were right at the top. They—we—were the strongest, which made Balor the strongest of the strongest.

And now, he was standing in my flat, glaring at me with that unnerving glittering eye of his.

"I would ask you if you want to come in, but you're already inside," I said, unable to keep the snark out of my tone. Despite the fact that he kind of terrified me, I couldn't help but throw some attitude his way. Other fae might bend to his will, but that was something I would never do.

"You were harder to find than I thought you'd be," he said, his lips curling up into a delicious smile that sent a thrill down my spine. And then he flicked his gaze around, frowned. "I have to admit that I didn't expect your lodgings to be quite this..."

He left off the last word, but he didn't need to say more than that. My flat was a wreck, but even then, it was a hole in the wall and the only place I could afford.

"Luckily for you, you'll be coming with me now. To my Court." His gaze narrowed; my heart tripped.

I couldn't go with Balor to his Court. It would only be so long until he—and the other fae—would realise who I was. The only way to keep myself alive was to stay on my own, out of sight and out of mind.

"Clark?" a small, familiar old voice whispered into my flat just as an elderly man hobbled through the doorway. He took one look at Balor and rolled his eyes. "Clark, love. We need to have a bit of a chat. I've given you as many chances as I can. It's time for you to move out."

2

"Hi, Henry," I said, shooting my old landlord a tight smile and wishing I could shoo both him and Balor away with my mind. But while I could read thoughts, I definitely couldn't control them.

Unfortunately.

"Clark, love. I thought we discussed this." He gestured around my living room slash home office and frowned. "You only just got things repaired after your last supernatural fight here."

"I know, Henry." I blew out a hot breath, dropping my eyes to the mess. The desk was in pieces, and slivers of wood were scattered all across the floor. My heart squeezed tight. The thing was, I couldn't blame Henry for wanting me out of here. He'd given me more than enough chances. I just…I needed one more. As much as I hated to do it, I was going to have to appeal to the human side of him, the caring side. "But you know I have nowhere else to go. I'll get all this cleaned up. And you know I'll take care of the dents in the walls eventually. Everything will be nice and shiny in a few days."

"I don't doubt it," he said with a slow nod. For a moment, I thought he'd let this go. Again. For the hundredth time. But then he pressed his lips together, and my heart dropped. "I'm afraid it's more than just the damage though, Clark. The other tenants, you know they're human. They've banded together to form some kind of council, and they're all threatening to leave the building unless you're out. Losing all that rent is a blow I just can't afford. I'll give you a week to get your things moved somewhere else."

All the blood drained from my face. "I have nowhere to go, Henry."

I'd known the humans weren't happy with me. Hell, I could hear it from their thoughts every time I passed one of them in the hall. But I hadn't known it was *this* bad. A week?! That was criminal.

"I'm sorry, Clark." He took a step back, shaking his head and casting his eyes to the ground as if he couldn't bear to look at me. "Don't you have friends you can stay with? Family?"

His words were like a slap in the face. "No."

"Well, if you want me to help you pack things up, I'll be downstairs." He took one last gaze around the room. "Probably best not to move in with any other supernaturals. Not if they're all like this."

～

It took me a moment to catch my breath. Henry had been threatening to kick me out for months now, but he'd never gone through with it. I knew he had a soft spot for me, even if he didn't approve of what I did or who my clients were. But the other tenants had pushed him to a decision that had turned my whole life upside down.

That was why it took me a few minutes to realise that Balor was gone. Just...gone. At some point during my conversation with my landlord, he'd slunk out of my office. Or vanished into thin air. I didn't know what his power was other than that whole flaming eye business of his.

To be honest, I was kind of surprised. Me getting kicked out of my flat seemed like the kind of thing he'd be all smug about. Not to mention the fact that he'd been two seconds away from throwing me over his shoulder and taking me straight to his Court, kicking and screaming.

Where had he gone? And why? More importantly, when would he be back?

With a heavy sigh, I pulled my long red hair into a high ponytail and pushed through the door to my bedroom. It was a tiny space with a single window that looked out at the concrete building next door. I had a thin slice of a bed that I'd smashed up against a desk that I used to hold my podcasting equipment: a microphone, a headset, and an old laptop that ran slower than an Uber during London's rush hour.

The walls were a strange shade of yellow, and the ceiling overhead bubbled from a leak on the floor above. Truth be told, my place was a dump. A gross, dilapidated dump. But it was *my* place. I'd lived here for two years. It had become my home.

That said, even if Henry *hadn't* decided to kick me out, the time had come for me to get the hell out of here. And not in a week. *Now.* Balor Beimnech, the Prince of the Crimson Court, had found me. He might have left during my argument with Henry, but he'd be back. And there was no telling when. It could be next week. It could be tomorrow. Or it could be tonight. I couldn't be here when he returned.

He would force me to join his Court, and then it would only be a matter of time before he discovered the full truth of me and my past.

My grandmother had sent me away from America ten years ago. To keep me safe. To keep me hidden from Faerie. She'd sacrificed so much so that I could stay hidden. I couldn't let her sacrifices go to waste.

I had to get out of here.

With a heavy heart, I grabbed a small rucksack and threw in a few changes of clothes, taking a sad glance at my podcasting equipment I'd have to leave behind. I didn't know how long I would be on the run without a home. It would only be extra dead weight. And it wasn't like I'd be able to record any episodes until I found somewhere else to live.

I could come back for it later...

I just needed to check my email one last time.

Glancing at the open door, I grabbed my laptop and flipped open the screen, quickly scanning my inbox. There were two dozen messages from listeners, a question from a potential sponsor I was desperate to snag, and one curious email from Ondine.

Ondine was a fae and one of my only friends in

the world. She also happened to be my mole inside the Crimson Court. Even though she served Balor, she didn't fully trust him. Balor had...a reputation of sorts. For violence, for fury, and for being The Most Eligible Supernatural Bachelor in the world. He fully enjoyed his status, rotating through a cast of pretty brunettes. Humans, fae, and otherwise. So, when two brunettes had gone missing from his House, Ondine had suspected that he might be the one behind it.

And then she'd come to me.

The email was short, but it was enough to pique my interest: *I've found out more about the missing females. Meet me in our usual spot at 10 tonight.*

Our usual spot was the pavement underneath Big Ben.

I glanced at the clock on my laptop. It was twenty to ten now. With a quick breath, I nibbled on my bottom lip, my heart now torn in two. Meeting Ondine was a terrible idea. If Balor came back here and found I was gone, he would most likely go looking for me. I needed to get out of London and *fast*. The area around Big Ben was extremely populated, which meant that a lot of eyes would be on me. At the same time, even Balor couldn't abduct someone in the middle of the streets around Parliament.

And I'd promised to help Ondine, no matter what.

"Fine," I muttered to myself. "One quick trip to meet Ondine, and then I'm gone."

It was the middle of January and London was freezing. Everyone was packed into thick coats, woollen scarves, and bobble hats. Their breaths were white clouds of mist on the air, and the jostling rush to get through the crowd was much more insistent than usual. No one wanted to be outside right now.

Hell, I didn't either.

As I stood on the pavement just down the street from Parliament, Big Ben began to chime. I'd barely made it over from East London in time to meet up with Ondine, but I'd somehow managed to beat her here. There was no sign of her. Not yet.

The bustling crowd was one of the reasons we picked this location. No one would pay much attention to us with so many people around, and supernaturals didn't tend to roam around here too much. Sure, sometimes our leaders met with members of Parliament, but that didn't tend to happen here. The MPs preferred to keep any meetings with supes away from the public eye. Humans were distrustful of us. Not that I could blame them.

More people bustled by. More buses rumbled down the street. Frowning, I turned to glance up at the looming clock behind me. It was already twenty past, and Ondine had been a no show.

That wasn't like her. Ondine tended to be early. She liked to-do lists and check boxes and tailored clothes.

After Balor's impromptu visit, I kind of felt a little twitchy about her absence. Had he tracked me down *through* her? Of course, she'd never been to my flat, nor did she even know where it was. I'd made sure to keep those details hidden, just in case. Still, he could have found out that she'd been snitching to me. Maybe someone had read her thoughts. I didn't know any other mind readers personally, but I knew I couldn't be the only one in London.

Dread began to creep down my spine. If Balor had found out Ondine and I were friends, then he might very well be on his way here now.

My palms felt sweaty in my gloves. I glanced at every face that passed me by, expecting every single freezing human to transform into Balor's tall, commanding form with his perfectly-sculpted face and blazing red eye.

I took one last glance over my shoulder at Big Ben's copper frame. I'd been waiting almost half an hour now, and Ondine had never been late before. She probably wasn't going to show. I hated to let her down on the slim chance that she was just running late, but I'd be a hell of a lot less useful to her if I got caught.

Sucking the wintry air into my lungs, I hunkered down into my thick scarf and turned away from Parliament. Just as I'd taken two steps down the pavement, a heavy hand landed on my shoulder. A hand much heavier than Ondine's. My entire body froze, heart tripping in my chest. A sliver of ice slid down my spine, and I curled my hands into fists. More to keep myself steady than because they'd do any good.

When I whirled on my feet, I expected to see Balor standing just before me. And well, maybe I did? It was impossible to tell. Whoever stood before me was very much fae. Of that much I was certain. He—or she—

was tall and lithe and power radiated off him in waves. But everything else about his body was hidden beneath a thick black coat and heavy boots. A mask topped it off, obscuring his face.

I narrowed my eyes and took a step back, jostling into a passing human. "Is this really necessary, Balor? I know you're not supposed to show up at Parliament, but your little burglary disguise here is a bit much, don't you think?"

In fact, it was weird as hell. Balor was the kind of fae who liked to be seen. He'd even opened a club in Soho a few years ago to profit off his popularity. He attended every Saturday night, holing himself up in a glass-encased platform above the dance floor so that humans—and supes—could gape at him and his VIP buddies. Most of the time, he invited girls up there, too.

So, why the hell was he wearing a mask?

Of course, he didn't deem my question important enough to answer. Instead, he angled closer to me, his body towering over my unimpressive five foot two. I wet my lips and glanced around. Surely he wasn't going to try to abduct me in front of all these humans.

"Look, I know you're pretty insistent I go with you to your Court, but I swear I'll start screaming if you lay another hand on me." I squared my shoulders and took a deep breath, trying to show him that I meant business.

Unfortunately, my little threat was meaningless to him.

He lifted his arms from his side, curling his right hand into a trembling fist. Magic stormed through the hushed street, humans slowing to stare open-mouthed at this outright display of fae power. I shuddered at the strength of it, swallowing hard and taking another step back.

But it was too late. The bright golden magic formed a ball in Balor's hand, and then he punched me right in the face.

The world disappeared out from under me.

3

My entire body felt like it had been run over by a truck. Groaning, I cracked open my eyes to find Balor freaking Beimnech staring down at me with an amused glint in his single red eye. Irritation stormed through me. And anger. Who the hell did he think he was, taking me out in the middle of London's streets?

What he had done was probably against some kind of supernatural law. Problem was, Balor was kind of the maker of laws. So, that didn't help me much.

"Good morning, Clark." He shot me a glittering smile that made my toes curl in my socks. I blinked. I was only wearing socks. That meant Balor had taken off my boots. Annoyingly, I didn't find myself as mad about that as I should have been. Quickly, I mentally checked the rest of my clothes. All there.

When I didn't answer, he said, "It's about time you woke up."

I narrowed my eyes. "Screw you."

He arched a brow. "Interesting. I assumed you would be thanking me."

Oh, right. Because I was a Courtless fae who had been 'rescued' from having to live her life in blissful solitude without the ever-present horrible thoughts from so-called friends who were supposed to care (but never truly did). Most fae probably *would* thank Balor for knocking them out. I, on the other hand, refused to be that pliable.

"Maybe I'd be thanking you if you hadn't decided to knock me senseless in front of half of London. Plus, I feel like shit, so whatever spell you cast on me clearly did some damage."

Was this what he'd done to those missing fae? I might have actually been scared he was doing the same to me, but I knew I wasn't his type. He liked brunettes, ones that were taller, prettier, and who probably didn't feel the need to eat ten times a day (thanks, shifter hunger).

In fact, as I glanced around, I could see that I wasn't in some sort of evil murder den. Instead, it looked suspiciously like a human hospital room. I was in a small, comfortable bed covered in white linen and surrounded by a couple of sterile metal tables. There was even a stethoscope on one. Just over Balor's shoulder, a female fae with silver hair stood wringing her hands.

Balor's face clouded over. "You truly believe that *I* attacked you."

"Er..." I frowned. "Well, yeah. Who else would it have been? You showed up at my flat demanding that I go to your Court. Instead, I went to Big Ben where someone attacked me, and now I wake up here. Are you telling me that wasn't you who knocked me out?"

With an irritated sigh, he stood and crossed his arms over his chest. "Of course it wasn't me. In fact, I risked losing the attacker in order to get you back here safely."

He stared down at me, his red eye glittering with emotion. Truth was, I didn't believe him for one bloody second. It was kind of a coincidence, was it not? He just so happened to *lose the fae* who attacked me. And, this was the kicker, he'd been near Big Ben at precisely the right second to save the day.

Right. I wasn't born yesterday, Balor the smiter.

"Your timing is certainly...lucky," I said dryly. "You know, that you just so happened to be near Parliament right as I was getting attacked."

If only I could read his mind and be certain of my hunch.

"It wasn't lucky," he said. "I followed you from your flat. It looked as though you were on a mission, potentially meeting with someone with the way you kept checking the time. I wanted to see who."

Interesting. So, he didn't know that I'd been on my way to meet Ondine. This was a good thing. If he didn't know about her, then she was still safe. Me, on the other hand...

"No, I was just out for a stroll," I chirped, glancing at the fae who still stood behind him, wringing her hands together. "Now, if you'll excuse me, I'll just be getting on out of here."

Balor pushed me firmly back onto the bed when I started to rise, his fingers brushing against the exposed skin of my shoulder. I did my best not to shudder, but...I failed. As terrifying and as cruel as he was, there was no denying that he was pretty much the hottest guy I'd ever laid eyes on. Not that I would let him know that. Thank the gods that *I* was the mind-reader, not him.

"You will not be leaving," he said with a frown. "You said that you're in pain. Deirdre here will heal you, and then you will join my Court."

Dammit. I'd kind of hoped that he'd forgotten about that whole joining his Court thing. He didn't seem like the kind of fae prince that would take no for an answer. But I had a sneaking suspicion that it was already too late. This might look like a human hospital, but that nurse or doctor was very much not human.

"You've already taken me to your Court," I said in a flat voice. "Haven't you?"

That meant I was inside the recently-renovated Battersea Power Station on the south side of the River Thames, a massive brick building that housed a couple hundred fae. Rumors suggested Balor Beimnech had spent seventeen billion pounds to turn the place into his Courtly home.

Even though Balor had claimed to have 'saved' me from my 'attacker' on the streets, he'd still abducted me anyway. He'd plucked me right out of my life and dropped me into his, all without asking my opinion on the whole thing.

It would have been easy. All it would have taken was a: *Hey, Clark. Would you like to join the Crimson Court?* That would have been the polite thing to do.

He arched an eyebrow. "I damn well didn't take you anywhere else. As far as I can tell, you have no home. Don't tell me your landlord changed his mind about evicting you from that dirty hole you called a flat."

I curled my hands around the sheets and shot him a glare. "Well, aren't you rude."

"Tell me I'm wrong." A slight smile played across his lips. "Tell me you would rather live there than here, where all your needs are taken care of."

Well, I mean, yeah. That was a no-brainer. Of course I wanted to live in my dirty flat.

There were three massive problems with his assumption. First, I didn't want or need anyone else to take care of me, thank you very much. I was perfectly capable of doing that myself, just as I had been for years. The idea that he thought I needed to be *saved* burned through me like fire.

Second, I wasn't entirely sure I agreed with the whole Court system in the first place. It seemed archaic and suffocating. The fae separated themselves from the human population, hiding in their fancy houses and making laws that applied to the supernatural world as a whole. Humans knew about us now. There was no reason to stand apart anymore.

And third...well, like I'd said, there were details about my past that would get me into a hell of a lot of trouble with not only Balor but with everyone else. They would likely want me dead.

Personally, I liked living, even if it sucked a lot of the time.

Unfortunately, most fae wouldn't react the way I

was reacting. They'd be excited about pledging their allegiance to this Court. Resisting would only raise red flags. So, out of pure self-preservation, I needed to lie.

"It's not that I don't want to live here. It's just...that flat became my home, even if it wasn't the greatest living situation in the world. I've spent a hell of a lot of time there. It's where I work. It's where I sleep."

It's where I make a podcast about supernatural drama...

"Trust me. You'll like it here much better." He flashed me that strange, hypnotic, disarming smile of his, and I couldn't help but shudder in response. A reaction that I could tell pleased him by the jackass wink he shot me.

"Yes. I'm sure I will be very happy." *As soon as I get the hell out of here.*

"As soon as you're fully healed, you'll stand trial." Balor stood and laced his hands behind his back, giving a no-nonsense nod to the female behind him. "There's no time to waste. We must solidify your place in this Court and determine your House immediately. Things are...uneasy, at the moment. As you know, several female fae of my House have recently gone missing. Another has disappeared this week."

All the blood drained from my face. "What are you talking about? Another one's gone?"

I didn't even ask him how he knew that I was privy to that information. If he'd found my flat, he'd definitely found out about my podcast. I'd been rambling on about the disappearances for days.

"Yes." He pressed his lips tightly together. "A female named Ondine."

I gasped, my stomach clenching tight. *No.* My mind raged against itself, trying to reject Balor's words, even though they made perfect sense. Ondine had been snooping around, and she'd found something. She'd sent me an email to meet her by Big Ben, but the abductor—Balor, probably—had gotten to her first.

And here I was, sitting in his lair.

"What if I don't want to join your Court?" The words popped out of my mouth before I could stop them.

He narrowed his eyes, leaned down to stare right into my face. I shivered at the intensity of his gaze. He might only have one eye on display, but it was unnerving as hell, and it left my entire body impossibly weak. I swallowed hard, wet my lips.

He practically growled.

Whoops. I definitely shouldn't have said that.

"No fae wants to be Courtless," he practically spat. "Why are you resisting? Why do you keep running from me?"

And the unspoken question: *what are you hiding?*

It was clear I was between a rock and a very hard place. And no, I didn't mean his abs of steel. I had two choices, neither of which were particularly great. I could either try to fight my way out of here and run off into the wilds where I'd have no chance of finding out what happened to Ondine, even though it would mean I was safe—kind of. He'd likely still try to track me down. Or, I could stay here, join his Court, and get the inside scoop by lurking around as much as possible. Bonus: Balor would stop being suspicious of me.

I ground my teeth together, fighting to keep my every emotion and thought from flying across my face. If only I could read his mind and know exactly what he was thinking. For a moment, I didn't say a word, focusing my efforts on probing his mind, but it was no use. There was no breaking through whatever mental barriers he'd erected.

"You're kind of infamous," I said, fumbling for an answer that would make sense to him. "Rumor has it that you're kind of...well, a hard-ass who isn't afraid to get violent. And your eye. Apparently, if you look at someone, they'll burst into flames. Humans are both intrigued by you and terrified to get near you. How can you blame me for running?"

His single eye softened. It caught me off guard, to be honest. I thought he'd be smug about his reputation. He liked to fan the flames (pun intended) as much as possible. "I do not get violent with my own Court members, which you will become. So, you have no reason to fear me."

Inwardly, I groaned. There wasn't any way out of this one. I would have to do his stupid trial. I would have to join his stupid Court. At least it would give me a chance to find out what had happened to Ondine, and then I'd get the hell out of here.

After a moment, I gave a nod, and his eye flickered with triumph. There was the smug expression I'd been expecting. It made me want to punch him, but it probably wasn't a good look, throwing my fist at my future Prince.

He gave a nod toward the nurse and drifted toward the door, throwing one last glance over his shoulder before he left the room. "One more thing.

No more podcasting. You'll be assigned a job, chosen by me."

"But—"

He held up a hand. "No objections. I've made up my mind. Now, get some rest. Your trial will take place first thing in the morning."

4

By the time the sunlight streamed in through the small window of my healing room, I'd already been awake for several hours. Who the hell could sleep knowing they were about to face some kind of terrifying trial to join a Court full of crazy fae? I mean, I assumed they were crazy. I hadn't spent much time around fae myself, but I'd heard enough stories to get an idea of what they were like as a group.

Powerful and terrifying.

A knock sounded on the door, but the female guard who strode inside didn't wait for me to respond before she barged right on through. She was almost as tall as Balor, and her golden hair was tied up in a high ponytail that swished as she moved. She had a belt slung around her waist, complete with a sheathed sword that matched her black ensemble. Her thick leather boots were definitely made for kicking ass.

She flicked her eyes up and down my faded jeans and frowned. "You look like a human."

"Thanks?" I raised an eyebrow as she shoved a black package into my hands. It had a satin bow tied around it, and the box felt strangely heavy.

"Not a compliment." The guard—at least, that was what I assumed she was in her sword-toting outfit—gave a curt nod at the box. "Get changed. Someone will be coming to do something about your hair. And then I'll escort you to your trial."

"Changed?" I untied the box and let the ribbon fall to the ground. When I peeked inside, I swore underneath my breath. Inside, there was a slinky black dress with straps that were thinner than string. The material was wispy, and I could tell just by looking at it, that the dress would barely hit mid-thigh. "Um, what kind of trial is this? Please don't tell me it involves some kind of sex ritual."

With Balor. My cheeks flamed just thinking about it.

The guard snorted. "You wish. No, this is just tradition. These kinds of ceremonies don't happen very often. We rarely stumble upon a Courtless fae who isn't Courtless because they've been banished. So, it's a pretty big deal. The whole Court will be there. We all dress up. You, especially."

I lifted an eyebrow and pointed at her black trousers. "You're not dressed up."

"I'm a guard. Guards don't wear pretty dresses." She stuck out a hand and smiled. "Name's Moira."

I took her hand in mine and shook it. Strong, purposeful, confident, totally no-nonsense. Right then and there, I decided Moira and I would get along. "I'm Clark."

"So Balor said. He's been looking for you for weeks now, you know."

I tried not to visibly cringe. As crazy as it sounded, I had kind of hoped he'd kept the details of our little run-in to himself. The moment we'd met had been charged, and I may or may not have kneed him in the balls. I would have preferred for no one else to know about that, but of course he would have told his guards.

Moira didn't seem too pissed off about it though, so maybe it wouldn't be as mortifying as I thought.

"I've never been part of a Court," I said by way of explanation. "His reputation kind of scared me."

"You don't look scared." She cracked a grin and stepped closer. My heart began to tremble. Had she guessed the truth? "Here's what I think. You knew that if he found out about your podcast, he'd be miffed and refuse to let you carry on with it. Am I right?"

I blew out a hot breath. Sure, we could go with that. Far better than the truth. "Would you blame me? He's shut that thing down already. I'm not allowed to podcast anymore, according to him. Instead, he's giving me some other job."

"If I were you, I'd stick to that," she said with a curt nod. "Balor is an amazing Prince. He looks after us, and he'd do anything for this House and the Court as a whole. But, he's big on honesty. He hates being betrayed. Go against him, and you'll only end up experiencing his wrath."

Wrath? I inwardly rolled my eyes. Yeah. He sounded *totally* amazing.

"But look on the bright side," she said with a smile. "He'll give you a proper job working for the Court."

"Yeah," I said, trying and failing to sound upbeat about it. Truth was, I liked investigating supernatural issues and reporting on them. Sure, some of them were kind of lame, like the whole werewolf cheating case that had landed me in this mess in the first place. But mostly, I liked it. Partly because I was pretty damn good at it, thanks to my mind reading gift. "I guess traipsing around in a dress all day hasn't ever been high on my list of priorities."

"Oh, that?" Moira waved her hand at the flimsy dress. "That's only for tonight. Once you get your job assignment, you'll be given an actual uniform."

Well, I guess there was one plus in a very empty column that sat next to a minus column that was practically never-ending.

"Anyway, time to get dressed," Moira said after glancing at a watch on her wrist. "Balor expects you to be in the Throne Room in half an hour, and he's not a fan of late arrivals."

Of course he wasn't. I'd only just met the guy, but I could already tell he had a stick up his ass.

Moira half-turned, then tossed the next words over her shoulder. "Sorry to stand watch like this while you're getting dressed, but...well, Balor insisted. He thinks you're a bit of a flight risk."

He wasn't wrong about that. Damn him for being too smart for my own good.

With a heavy sigh, I slipped out of my trousers and blouse and shimmied the silky black dress over my head. It fit me like a glove, which begged the question: how the hell did Balor know my size? I shuddered. Maybe I didn't want to know the answer to that question.

Had he merely guessed? Or had he snuck into my bedroom to check my clothes? That was pretty creepy no matter which way I looked at it. Another point in the "potential abductor" column for Balor, Prince of London's fae.

The door cracked open again just as I was slipping my feet into a pair of heels that could have easily doubled as torture devices. Damn did they pinch my toes.

The new arrival was another female. She had long silver hair that hit her waist, a tiny nose, and the biggest pair of silver eyes I'd ever seen. Her pointed ears poked through her smooth hair. She'd pierced them, and two tiny stars clung to the points.

"Hi there, Clark," she said in a bubbly voice. "My name is Elise, and I'm the one who will be glamouring you today."

"Hold up." I stopped fiddling with the skinny dress strap. "Did you just say glamouring me? Like, making me look like something else?"

Glamouring was another one of those things I'd heard a lot about, but I'd never seen for myself, at least that I knew of. It was totally possible a fae had been glamoured around me before, and I'd had no idea. It completely transformed anyone's appearance. It wasn't a power I personally had access to, and my grandmother hadn't either.

So, this was new. But also, why the hell was she going to glamour *me*?

Elise's face scrunched up, her tiny little nose transforming into something you might see on a bulldog. "Yeah, of course. Don't you know how the trial works?"

"That would be a no," I said slowly, feeling my neck twitch from the anxious beat of my heart.

"Don't worry," she said with a wave of dismissal, as if people went around being glamoured every day like it was no big deal. And...did they? There was a lot about the Courts I didn't know.

"It's nothing to be concerned about. You won't feel a thing. All you need to know is that you will be glamoured, and your true face—not your body—will be hidden from the Court. During the trial, your true face will be revealed *only* to the Master of your appointed House. That's how you find out where you belong."

"My appointed House." Dammit, I felt like an idiot. I had no idea what any of this meant.

Elise gave me a kind smile. "There are many Houses that are part of the Crimson Court." Okay, that I knew. "But there are only four within the United Kingdom. Since you were found here in London, you will be appointed to one of those. Personally, I think Balor is hoping you'll end up staying here at House Beimnech, even though he'll be your Prince no matter what."

I wet my lips. I wasn't entirely sure I liked the idea of Balor wanting me to stick around. "What makes you say that?"

"You're the first Courtless fae he's seen in awhile, and he has no idea where you've come from. I think you intrigue him."

Great. Just what I needed. The prince fae's eyes firmly pointed in my direction.

"Well, that makes two of us," I said quickly. "I

don't know where I came from either. I ended up out on my own when I was just a kid."

Lies. Total lies. I'd lived with my grandmother—secretly—until I was fifteen. Then, when she thought the Silver Court in America had begun to suspect something was up, she'd sent me here, to hide unseen in London's streets. That had worked for ten years. Until I'd made the mistake of snagging the attention of the wrong fae.

"Hmm. Well, Balor will find out. He always does."

Shivers coursed along my skin. I couldn't let that happen. He would kill me. They'd all probably want to kill me. I'd be hung up in front of the entire Crimson Court while every single fae lobbed a rock at my head.

Sure, it had been years since they'd enacted that kind of punishment, but…

"Anyway, you'll be in Balor's Court regardless, so he'll have time enough to look into your past." Elise gave a smile and a nod. "It'll be fun to see where you're meant to end up."

Fun. She and I had very different definitions of that word.

5

When I stepped into the Throne Room, hundreds of eyes turned my way. I shifted on my feet, the tight high heels pinching my toes. I didn't feel like myself, and I knew I looked like an entirely different fae due to Elise's little glamouring spell. She hadn't shown me my new face, but I *felt* different, like a strange second skin had been pressed on top of mine. The back of my neck prickled, both from the intense power that charged through the room and from the cold. It was winter, and no way in hell this Throne Room had heat.

The lofted ceiling rose high above, intricate designs painted across the domed surface. Chandeliers hung low from metal ropes, and a long, red carpet had been stretched out on the floor before me. It led straight up to the platform ahead where Balor sat on a throne made of hundreds of crimson skulls.

I swallowed hard. No one could say this fae wasn't morbid.

"Come," he called out and waved his hand, a signal for me to move forward.

I glanced to his left and his right before making a move. There were three other Masters beside him. Two females, one male. All decked in royal finery. They sat in tall gold chairs that were elaborately carved with shapes of daggers and arrows. They, I assumed, were the Masters of the other Houses. One from Wales, one from Scotland, and one from Ireland.

One of these four fae would become my leader within only a moment's time.

They would rule me. And I'd never met a single one of them before in my life.

Well, except for Balor, and I didn't know if what we had shared could be called actual *meetings*. Awkward and terrifying run-ins, maybe. One where he may or may not have knocked me unconscious. And one where I'd definitely kneed him in the freaking prince balls.

Wobbling in my heels, I took slow and very unsteady footsteps down the carpet. A few sniggers echoed through the lofted hall, and I shot daggers at the culprit. A burly male fae hidden amongst the crowd at the edge of the carpet. I rolled my eyes. But of course. He would have no idea how impossible heels were. I could kill Balor when all of this was over for subjecting me to this kind of embarrassment. It was bad enough that I was being forced to join his Court but also having to do it in heels?

Asshole.

When I reached the end of the carpet, I stopped and looked expectantly at Balor. He sat on his throne, lounging back with a smug, bored expression on his face. It made me want to slap him even harder than I'd wanted to before, and that was saying something.

"Hello, Clark. This is your official welcome to the Crimson Court," he said with that strange, unsettling smile of his. "You were once Courtless, but no more. You will join our ranks. You will swear fealty to your Master, and you will support your brethren with every breath you take. You will honour us, and you will defend us. Do you agree?"

My heart roared in my chest as Balor leaned forward, lifting an eyebrow. I could tell he held his breath, curious to see how I would respond. Was this part of the trial? Some kind of test? Quietly, I cracked open the part of my mind that allowed me to listen in on the thoughts of others. Not too much. That would be chaos. There were hundreds of fae in this room, and that was far too many voices for one half-fae mind to handle.

Instead, I focused my ears on the fae sitting just to the right of Balor. He was quiet, his dark eyes and hair a match for the formal attire he wore. Rubbing his chin, he looked almost concerned, as if he didn't want me to join the Court. He was tall and thick, so large that he dwarfed the elaborate chair, the muscles in his body chiseled perfectly for war.

There is something different about her. No doubt Balor is eager for her to join his ranks. Once she swears fealty, she is bound to this Court forever.

Bound to the Court forever? My heart hammered hard and my palms went slick. This was a little tidbit that Balor had neglected to mention. But what did it even mean? Bound to the Court? It sounded like some kind of vow, the kind that Knights made when agreeing to protect a King.

I couldn't make a vow to Balor or any of these other fae. I wouldn't be here very long. I refused to pledge my entire future to any of these Masters, any of these beings who would no doubt rather see me dead if they new the truth of me.

What would this mean for my eventual escape? Would I be able to leave? Or would my vow to these people—to these fae—somehow prevent me from getting the hell out of here?

Silence descended as I stared at Balor and as he stared at me. The entire Court was hanging on my every breath, waiting to see what words I would say next.

In an ideal world, I'd kick off these heels and stride right on out of here without looking back.

Unfortunately, this wasn't an ideal world. I saw no way of getting out of this one, not without causing a hell of a lot of drama I wasn't prepared to face. Hundreds of fae were watching me. There were guards at the door. I was in this fancy-ass, thin-as-hell dress, and I'd stumbled my way up the red carpet.

It wasn't like I could run. They would stop me if I tried.

Balor leaned further forward, his single eye piercing right into my soul. *"Do you agree, Clark?"*

Dammit.

"Yes," I puffed out the word, almost a whisper. "Yes, I agree."

Oh god, what have I done?

Something strange happened then. Well, something stranger than everything that had happened so far, but it had been one strange-ass week, I had to admit. Wind began to stir, and deep, dark magic began to slither along my skin. My chest went tight. Strands of silk caressed my neck, and the whisper of a breath tickled my ear. I sucked in a sharp breath and glanced up at Balor. He still lounged nonchalantly on his throne, but there was a spark in his eye that made it clear that he knew exactly what I felt.

And that he was behind it.

The magic whispered away, and the murmurs of the fae rose like a chorus of excitement. Whatever had just happened? It meant something. And I was pretty sure I didn't like whatever the hell it was. Was I bound to Balor now? And if so, could I get the hell out of it? Regardless of the magic, I would not be permanently bonded to *anyone*. Not even a shitty Prince.

Especially not a shitty Prince.

"Good." The ghost of a smile whispered across Balor's lips, and then he twitched his fingers toward a curtain of shadows off to the left of the throne. A form shifted out from the shadows, almost seemingly from thin air. A female fae with hair as dark as the deepest part of the night. She was tall and lithe, but her spine curved over as if the weight of the world rested on the back of her neck. Her eyes were dark and hollow, and her cheeks were as pale as a full moon's glow.

I knew who this was. I might be an outcast fae with little knowledge, but my grandmother had taught me a few important details. I knew the key players, and this female was one. This was Caer, the fae goddess of prophecy and dreams. She and her hollow black eyes were infamous. Caer could see visions, of the past, of the present, and of the future. Sometimes all three at once.

It also made her extremely unstable. Sometimes, she could go a bit mad. And now she was staring right at me.

"Clark, meet Caer," Balor said, his lips twisting into a smile when he saw the uneasy expression on my face. "She will look into your soul and read you. The depths of your being will reveal where you belong. And then your true face will be revealed to your new Master." A beat passed. "Of course, I have already seen your face even if I cannot see it now. You will be in my Court regardless. You just may not be in my House as well."

The other Masters shifted on their golden chairs, visibly annoyed by Balor's clear power grab. They might be the Masters of their Houses, but *he* was *their* Master.

I wet my lips. "What if my face isn't revealed to any of you?"

Balor narrowed his eye, and a murmur went through the crowd.

She's questioning him.

How dare she challenge the Prince.

Whispers and murmurs grew in the Throne Room. I had to shut my eyes to block out their voices. They were loud, loud, loud, echoing in my ears and making my head spin. I wiped my sweaty palms on my dress, cracking an eye to risk a glance at the Prince. He was staring at me with an extreme kind of intrigue that made me feel as though I were an insect underneath a microscope.

That was when I realised the voices weren't murmurs at all. It was happening in my head.

Yeah. That happened occasionally, and it sucked. Sometimes my mind had trouble piecing out what was real and what wasn't real. Well, kind of, anyway. The voices *were* real. They were thoughts and questions and repressed ideas, but they were silent. To everyone else but me.

And sometimes, I just found it kind of hard to know if a thought was spoken aloud or in someone's head.

Like I said, my faerie powers? Not really under my control.

I was pretty sure that had something to do with my Courtless status, which meant I might actually find some temporary relief while I was inside this Court.

If Balor didn't kill me first.

"Your soul is loud," Caer whispered, taking a step closer to me and placing a single trembling hand on the top of my head. Her touch was cold, and it sunk into my bones like the kind of chill you can't shake, no matter how long you sit beside the fire to get warm again. I held back a shiver and met her gaze, but her vacant eyes only made the chill that much deeper.

Could she really see the future? And my past? If so…what did she see?

She closed her eyes, and that was when I felt as though I could truly see her. She was younger than she appeared. Probably four hundred years instead of the thousands I would have guessed before. On the outside, she was haunting, terrifying, and more than a teensy bit creepy. But on the inside? She was broken. Scared. Small.

"There is more to you than meets the eye," she murmured, practically parroting what I'd heard the Master think. A chill swept down my spine. Had she heard that from him, too? Or was that something she actually saw in me? Either way...we needed to get this over with. Stat.

It was one thing dressing up in a too-tight dress and cramping heels. And it was one thing to stand here like a total idiot in front of hundreds of strangers, a monkey in the zoo. And it was one thing to be glamoured into a totally foreign face.

But, and this was the kicker for me, it was quite another thing entirely to feel as though my entire being was exposed to this female who could clearly see far more than was safe. Her eyes pierced into the very heart of me, and she knew. There was no doubt in my mind that she saw everything I'd spent my entire life trying to hide.

Who I was. Where I'd come from.

And what Balor would do if he found out himself.

She sucked in a sharp breath and stepped back, and then the window into her soul that she'd opened to me shut with a sharp snap. Those haunted black eyes of hers were back.

"The decision has been made."

She whirled toward the four Masters, one on his throne and three on their golden chairs. Gesturing at me, who stood behind her, with my heart hammering so hard that I could feel it in my bones, she said, "Clark, your Master, the only one who can see through the glamour, will now rise."

Balor rose with a terrifying smile.

6

*O*f course, it was always going to be Balor. I'd been an idiot to hope for anything else. Also? I was pretty sure that Caer wasn't reading some kind of almighty fated order from above. She'd merely seen my past and had decided to throw me into the lion's den.

Damn faeries.

Balor stood, his eye flashing as he lifted his chin. He looked as though he'd won a prize, as if he'd somehow beaten the other Masters who sat clustered around him. To be fair, all three of them were frowning, and the Master whose mind I'd read let out an exasperated sigh.

"Your fates and your futures are entwined," Caer said before casting one last look at me over her shoulder. Then, she turned and whispered back toward the corner from where she'd appeared. A second later, I could have sworn she'd become one with the dark curtains themselves.

With a roll of my eyes, I turned back toward Balor,

shifting in the pointy heels. What the hell was I supposed to do now? Curtsy or something? Well, if he thought I was going to get down on my knees and worship him like some kind of Greek God (even though he looked like one), he had another think coming.

But Balor's machismo had vanished. He stood staring after Caer, frowning.

She's never said anything like that before, came a whispered voice into my ear, murmuring to me from the gathered crowd.

I wonder what that meant. Could they be future mates?

I ground my teeth together and bit back a retort that would reveal my power to the whole damn room. Now, there wasn't inherently anything *wrong* with my power, per se. And it wasn't as though it would reveal who I was. Plenty of faeries could read minds.

Okay, so maybe not plenty. A few could. A very small few.

The point was, mind reading wasn't a super rare thing in the world of the fae, but that wouldn't stop anyone from freaking the fuck out. Mind readers weren't particularly popular, and I'd give you one guess why. No one wants their thoughts read. No one. And I wasn't about to start announcing it to all of these strangers. Strangers who I would now be living with every single damn day until I escaped. And that could take months. They already thought I was a weirdo. Partly for being Courtless, partly for challenging Balor, and partly because of Caer's strange words.

But all of that didn't stop me from wanting to

argue with them. They assumed I would end up as *Balor's mate*.

I mean, come on. I was my own person, dammit. I wasn't *anyone's* mate. And I especially wasn't his.

Balor moved through the crowd. Anyone who wasn't standing now clambered to their feet. "The trial is now over. Thank you all for coming. Feel free to enjoy the celebration for the rest of the evening. As is tradition, Clark will not be taking part. I'll show her to her room."

Not taking part in my own damn celebration? I'd be pissed off if I actually wanted to be a part of this Court, but I was kind of relieved I wouldn't have to play nice with hundreds of fae. My mind was already weary from the half hour I'd been in here. I could kind of use the rest, even though I wouldn't admit it to Balor's face.

Balor the smiter. My new Master. Ugh.

"Come," Balor said without a single glance my way. He beckoned me to follow him with a flick of his fingers, and then moved through the crowd like an angel of death.

I scowled at his back, but I followed after like the good little fae I was supposed to pretend to be. When he led me out of the Throne Room and into the outside corridor, I finally opened my mouth with a retort. "Just out of curiosity, is that how things are going to be? You flick your fingers, and I follow?"

The muscles of his back rippled as he tensed. "I would hate to think you are challenging me again."

I rolled my eyes. "I'm asking a question. I've never lived in a Court, remember? I know a little bit about Faerie but not much. You're going to have to explain to me how things work around here, or I'll only end up sticking my foot in my mouth."

"Speaking of your feet," he said smoothly, expertly dodging my questions. "You no longer need to wear those heels. I'll have some more comfortable boots delivered to your room, along with several sets of the standard uniform for our guards."

I stopped short and lifted a brow. "For your guards? You have seen me fight, yes? Or at least the remnants of that. I suck."

"Clark. Perhaps you should stop acting as though you just got thrown to the wolves. It makes it seem as though being in my House is the last thing you wanted." Finally, he turned toward me. But instead of continuing to speak, he grabbed my elbow and ushered me forward. "Trust me, you'll be happy about this. You'll be trained in combat, but I won't expect you to fight. You'll join the investigation team."

Right. He knew I'd been a PI in my Courtless life, and he was clearly hoping to capitalise on some kind of special investigatory abilities he probably assumed I had. Truth was, I was good at what I did, but the only way I ever solved a case was by flat-out reading everyone's minds. I didn't really have any skills beyond that.

That said, being on the investigation team would be a fast track to finding out what happened to Ondine. So, it wasn't all bad.

"Is it safe to assume that I'll be looking into the missing fae?" I asked.

He smiled. "I told you that you'd be happy about being in my House."

I had the sudden urge to punch the smirk right off his face, but I took solace in the fact that he had no idea that my first suspect? Him. And if he *was* the one behind the disappearances, I was determined to find the evidence.

"You do know that I am aware of your power, Clark."

His words came out of nowhere, like a slap in the face. Shit.

I pursed my lips, doing my best to put on a puzzled expression. "What ever do you mean?"

"You're smart to play it off. It's a dangerous gift. Many won't like what that means for them. Tell me, did you hear anything interesting in the Throne Room? Caer's words were quite curious. Did you gleam anything from her mind? Something that could explain what she meant?"

Shit, shit, shit. So, he really did know that I could read minds. But how? Ondine? Surely, she hadn't told him. In any other circumstance, I might wonder if Balor himself could read minds. But if he could, then this conversation would be going in an entirely different direction, and he wouldn't need me to tell him what Caer had thought.

Not that I'd been able to tell myself. I'd seen underneath her glamour, sure, but her mind was just as sharp as Balor's. Maybe even more so.

"Caer is clearly mad, but her mind, somehow, is a steel trap, and I have a sneaking suspicion that you already knew that." I let a beat pass before I said the next words. They weren't going to be a surprise to him either. Balor knew I could read minds, which meant that he must know I couldn't read his. "Just like yours."

"Ah." His eye flashed. "And there it is. I wondered

how long it would take you to bring it up. How badly has it been digging into your skin?" He leaned forward, placing one hand on the wall behind me. "My only question is, why did you try to read my mind that night at the club?"

I swallowed hard, wet my lips, and attempted to take a step back. And failed. My back hit the wall behind me, trapping me between it and Balor's thick, muscular chest. He was close. Too close. So close that I swore he could smell the fear thrumming in my neck.

"How did you know?" I whispered. "And why didn't you say anything about it until now?"

"You need to answer my questions first," he said with a grin. "I am the Master. And your Prince."

I fought the urge to roll my eyes. "One might wonder why you have to keep mentioning your authority. True rulers don't need to tell people who and what they are."

He let out a low growl, pushing closer, his chest now tightly pressed against mine. His heart hammered in his chest, almost in rhythm with my own. Power curled off his body, strands of his burning darkness brushing up against my skin. So it *had* been him earlier in the Throne Room. He'd used his power then, and he was using it again now. To remind me that I was subservient to him. To remind me that I had to obey.

I really didn't like obeying.

"You need to watch yourself," he finally said, taking a large step away from me. "I will excuse your attitude just this once, because you're new and you've just had your trial. But not again, Clark. I don't want to be forced to make an example out of you."

My heart thrummed in my chest, and I ached to

snark back. This time, though, I held my tongue. Not because I was bowing down to his authority, but because I knew I needed to play my cards right. If I pissed him off too much, I might find myself out on my ass and banished before I could look into Ondine's disappearance.

"Thank you, my Prince," I said in a syrupy sweet voice.

He narrowed his eye but argued no more. Instead, he whirled away from me and strode down the hallway without another word wasted on the newest annoying member of his Court. With a sigh, I followed after him. He led me up a flight of curving stairs toward a carpeted hallway highlighted with rich wood panelling. Old paintings hung in jagged lines, as if the decorator had randomly plopped them in any old place. Plus, there was a thick layer of dust on the tops of them. It kind of made the place feel less claustrophobic though. Not everything here had to be perfect and pristine, like the dozens of chandeliers, which I had to admit was a surprise.

"Your room will be here," he said when we reached the very end of the hallway. He pushed open a door, and with my breath held tight in my throat, I poked my head inside.

I didn't know what I'd expected. Chandeliers and claw-footed bathtubs. That or wooden floors painted with blood. Maybe both combined?

This was...well, it was kind of normal. Normal with a dash of absolutely breathtaking. There was a double bed on a black, wrought-iron frame, a cute little vintage bedside table, a line of empty shelves just above it, and a wardrobe that filled an entire wall. The windows went from the floor to the lofted ceiling, looking out at the glittering lights of nighttime London.

I tried not to make a strange gurgled impressed sound. I'm not sure if I succeeded.

I'd always wanted a view like this. The nighttime city lights always captivated me. It was one of the few things in the world that I'd ever truly *felt* deep down in my soul. When I saw the city sparkle, I felt alive.

"Good. I'm glad you like it," he said, sounding all smug and confident.

"Yeah, it's okay, I guess."

"A definite upgrade from your previous abode," he said with a sniff.

"Except my previous abode had my podcasting equipment and the freedom to record as many episodes as my heart desired," I said, unable to keep the words from popping out of my mouth.

His smile vanished. "It is essential that you understand I have given you an order, Clark. Disobey and there will be consequences."

"Yeah, you've made that much clear." I strode away from him, stood by the window, and peered outside. How the hell had I gotten here? Grandma would have lost her damn mind if she'd known exactly where I would end up. And she would have warned me, that despite this beautiful room, and despite this beautiful male, not to let down my guard.

I whirled toward Balor, and my heart thumped when I realised he'd closed the distance between us. "Thanks for the room. What happens now?"

"Now," he said, reaching out to push a strand of hair away from my face, "you settle in. I'll have someone bring you some clothes and details about your new assignment. You'll start working with my team first thing in the morning. Don't be late. And don't tell a single soul about your power. That's between you and me."

7

The next morning, Moira appeared outside my door at precisely six o'clock in the freaking morning. As a private investigator (and podcaster), I had a tendency to ere on the Night Owl end of the spectrum. Waking any hour before nine? Not really my thing.

So, you could say that I felt a little grumpy. Even more so when the realisation of exactly where I was sank into my sleep-addled brain. I wasn't waking in my gloomy East London flat in my tiny squashed bed by the window that looked out at a concrete wall. I was halfway across the city, stuck in a strange life as a new initiate into Balor's Court.

I rubbed my eyes and glared at Moira, even though I knew none of this was her fault. "This is an ungodly hour. Please don't tell me I have to get up now."

"Count yourself lucky. I had to get up at five." She tossed a chunk of black clothing at me and smiled. "That'll be your uniform most of the time. Technically, you're a part of the guard team, but you'll be on the investigation side rather than the security side. Still, you gotta wear the black wardrobe. Lucky for you, it's not a slinky dress."

"Let me guess," I said, flicking a glance toward the blade she kept in a golden belt slung around her waist. "You're the security side."

"Damn straight." She flashed a smile. "Though I don't see as much action as I used to back when supernaturals first came out to the world. Things have been pretty peaceful around here lately..." As she trailed off, her face clouded over. "Except for the missing fae. I'm guessing Balor filled you in?"

My heart thumped hard. The missing fae. The whole reason I was here. Suddenly, I felt a little more awake. "He told me a bit about them, but he didn't go into much detail. Apparently, my first assignment is helping out with that."

Moira gave a nod. "So he said. I have to admit it's a good fit. It's not every day we find a Courtless fae who also happens to be a trained private investigator."

Trained. Ha! I decided not to correct her. I wasn't trained in the slightest. The requirements for putting up my shingle had been incredibly minimal, particularly since I was focusing on clientele (scorned vampires and shifters, mostly) that most humans didn't want to touch with a ten-foot pole. Hell, make that a fifty-foot pole.

Even though supernaturals had come out to the world over ten years ago, humans weren't particularly comfortable with their existence. At the moment, we all lived in somewhat harmony, but there was tension brewing underneath the surface. I had no doubt that one day that tension would reach a boiling point. A spark would become a fire, one that couldn't be doused.

Moira moved to the door. "Alright, you've got your uniform now. This time, I'll leave you to get dressed in peace. I'll wait outside. You have ten minutes."

Ten minutes? I wrinkled my nose as she shut the door behind her, leaving me to the cocoon of my bed. My eyes were puffy, and my head was in some serious need of caffeine. I let out a heavy sigh and frowned down at my new uniform. It was pretty much identical to the outfit Moira wore. Black trousers, a black tank, and some black boots that looked as though they were made for kicking ass. On top of it all lay a smooth leather jacket. It was winter, after all.

Normally, I would take a warmish shower, dry my hair, and dab a little concealer on the bags around my eyes. One downside of being half-fae? I didn't have their naturally dewy skin regardless of the circumstances. If I was tired and sleep-deprived, it showed.

Unfortunately, I had less than ten minutes at this point, so a shower wasn't in the cards. With a roll of my eyes, I shimmied into the new ensemble. Once again, the clothes fit me like a glove, only this time, they were far more practical. And comfortable. I could definitely kick some ass in this. I mean, if I could actually kick ass in the first place. Which I couldn't.

Just as I was dabbing some concealer beneath my eyes, the door swung open. Moira raised her eyebrows when she saw what I was doing, but she didn't say a word.

"Two seconds, and I'm ready," I said. Dab, dab, dab, and I was done.

"Good. I hate to rush you. I know ten minutes isn't much, but Balor hates it when people are—"

"Late," I finished for her, stepping back from the mirror. My unwashed red hair flowed around my shoulders like a mess of fire, but at least I'd gotten rid of the purple bags under my eyes.

She bit back a smile. "Come on. The rest of the team are waiting for us."

~

Moira led me down two flights of stairs, and then through an archway that led to a second wing of the renovated power station. Where the first wing had felt homey and warm, this one felt far more utilitarian. There was no fancy carpet or chandeliers. That said, it was definitely as impressive, if not more so.

The ceilings rose high overhead, large open windows looking out at the dark sky above. Steel beams loomed in support. The floor was marble, and the dark stone glistened underneath the twinkling lights that hung from suspended chains. It was part-dungeon, part-warehouse, and part-Scotland Yard. There was a bank of computer stations along the far wall, and a massive whiteboard was propped up in the middle of the room. Names and identifying information had been scrawled across it in bright red marker. My eyes caught on Ondine's photo, and my breath caught.

Her familiar dark eyes, her long brown hair.

Suddenly, this whole thing felt far too real. Ondine

really was missing. And I was here to look into where she'd gone.

To find who had taken her.

Moira caught the look on my face and said, "Those are our missing girls. Three so far. It's been weeks since the first, Rosalind, went missing. We're trying to be optimistic, but…"

I cut my eyes her way, horrified to see the sadness in her expression. "What do you think has happened to them?"

"Honestly?" She raised her eyebrows and shook her head. "This kind of situation isn't really in our wheelhouse. Fae don't tend to get abducted, not when they're part of a Court. So, we've had to look to human experiences to get a feel for what might be going on."

She didn't elaborate, but I could fill in the blanks myself. The first seventy-two hours were crucial when humans went missing. The chances someone would be alive after that? Well, they weren't great.

"How long has Ondine been missing?" I asked.

"Only about twenty-four hours." Moira shot me a funny look. "How'd you know her name?"

I bit my tongue. None of these fae would be particularly happy if they found out Ondine had been a mole for me. Something told me that Balor might know, but he'd clearly kept that information to himself. I wanted to believe that Ondine was still alive. She'd only been missing for twenty-four hours, so there was still a good chance that we might be able to find her before anything terrible happened. And, if she was alive, I couldn't risk pissing off her fellow Court members.

"Balor mentioned it," I said with a noncommittal shrug.

I was saved from elaborating when the perky silver-haired fae from yesterday came bouncing up to us. Behind her, four more guards eyed me warily.

"Hey, Clark," Elise said. "Welcome to the team."

"I didn't realise you were one of the guards."

"Oh, I'm not really a guard," she said with a wave of her hand. "I'm an assistant, I guess you could say. Sometimes my glamouring skills come in handy."

That made sense. Balor had specifically picked me because of my powers. He probably picked the others for theirs, too. I glanced at the cluster of guards just behind her. Three males, one more female. Two of the males were bulky and menacing while one was skinny as a rail. The female had dark hair, a small waist, and cold hands apparently, if her gloves were any indication. She appeared to be the opposite of intimidating. Taller than me, of course, but *everyone* was taller than me. I couldn't help but wonder what skills each of these guards hid under their unassuming facades.

"This here is Duncan," Elise said, waving toward one of the bulkier guards. "He's the head of our team, and reports straight to Balor." She turned toward the skinnier of the males. "This is Kyle. He's only been here about a decade. And this here is Cormac and Lesley."

Lesley rolled her eyes.

"Just ignore her. She's used to having all the newbie attention and doesn't want to share," Elise said. "She transferred over from the Silver Court about five years ago."

"Transferred? That's a thing that can happen?"

The Silver Court. Hopefully, she wouldn't decide to ask me too many questions about my own time in America. My mind reached out in her direction, hoping to snatch one of her thoughts, but—

Elise lifted her shoulder in a shrug. "Only in exceptional circumstances. She came over here to get a degree from Oxford, and then decided to stay."

"Well, nice to meet you all," I said shifting on my feet. What was I supposed to do in this scenario? Bow? Or shake their hands? And did I shake Duncan's hand first? His scowl suggested…maybe not.

"As you can probably tell," Elise continued, "Duncan, Moira, Cormac, and Lesley operate as guards. Me and Kyle mostly do the investigations, so you'll be working with us."

Duncan cleared his throat and stepped forward. "You'll still be reporting to me. We all work as a team, as a unit, even if we have different focuses. And, when there is an event that requires it, we all work security. So, you will need to be trained for that."

"Like our seasonal parties," Elise added.

Ah, the infamous seasonal parties of the Courts. For some reason, I'd always assumed the parties were some kind of rumor or urban legend. On every solstice and every equinox, the entirety of every Court gathered together to celebrate the changing of the seasons. Rumors suggested they…tended to get pretty damn rowdy. Also, there was a lot of mating. Allegedly.

Hopefully I'd be long gone before I had to face the next one, set for the beginning of Spring.

"So…" I lifted an eyebrow. "Where do I start? What have you guys figured out so far?"

Kyle and Elise exchanged a look before motioning me over to the whiteboard. The rest of the team disappeared toward the other end of the expansive room, toward a table full of blades. They grabbed some weapons and headed out the door, no doubt to take up their stations as the security of this House.

Elise motioned at the information they'd gathered so far. Names, ages (like, seriously old ages), brief backgrounds, including where they'd lived in years past.

"As you can see, they all kind of…have similar features," Elise said. "Dark hair, pretty, relatively young for fae. All under a hundred."

I nodded, nibbling on my bottom lip. "Any of them have a boyfriend?"

Elise exchanged a glance with Kyle, who shook his head and said, "I've taken a look at their communications. No sign that they've been seeing anyone lately."

I levelled my gaze at him. "Are you seriously telling me you hacked their phones and their emails?"

"Well, yeah." His cheeks were dotted with pink. "They're missing."

That was a serious breach of confidentiality if there ever was one. I didn't like the idea that there was a hacker in the Court, one who could take a sneak peek into my private communications any time he wanted to. I'd have to make sure I didn't log in to my personal accounts while I was here. Otherwise, he would have full access to some pretty sensitive emails left over from my America days.

"Any other clues?"

Elise shook her head. "Only some hunches. Obviously, we think someone has taken them. The same someone. We've done our best to come up with a list of possibilities. Who are our enemies? We've never particularly gotten along with vampires or shifters, despite Balor's attempts at civility, but they don't tend to do this kind of thing. They're more…blatant. The vampires drain bodies of blood and leave them on display. Shifters aren't much better." She sucked in a deep breath before plowing forward. "So, that leaves us with the possibility that this could be coming from a rival Court."

"Or a rival *House*," Kyle said, emphasising the last word.

Chills swept down my spine. "You're saying a fae did this."

A fae, like Balor?

"We're saying that a fae *might* have something to do with it." Elise exchanged a glance with Kyle again. "But not just any fae. Most likely one who wants to challenge Balor. One who has long hated the idea of the red-eyed prince as the true ruler of the Crimson Court."

I shook my head, not quite understanding.

"We think that Fionn might have taken them," Kyle said. "The Master of House Futrail in Ireland. And if that's really the case then…well, London might just have a war on its hands."

8

After Kyle and Elise had filled me in on what little they had discovered in the three weeks that the fae had been missing, they showed me around what they dubbed the "command station" for the guards. There were some pretty impressive computers, which explained how Kyle was able to do his hacking thing, along with a sparring room through a door in the back corner.

They gave me a file with some more info and sent me along my way to break for lunch in the Court's five-star restaurant and do some reading. Apparently, my new job required homework. Yay.

On my way out the door, I passed Duncan. He was about twice as tall as me, but he felt ten times larger. He was one of those guys that just radiated strength and power, and I could understand why Balor had chosen him to be the leader of his security. I definitely wouldn't want to mess with him. When I finally escaped, I'd need to make sure I avoided breaking out during his shift.

"On your way to lunch?" he asked, face blank, eyes empty.

"Yes," I said slowly. "Is that a problem? I didn't have any breakfast, and I'm starving."

My half-shifter appetite meant I needed some food —and fast—or I would start getting a little cranky.

"No, go on," he said, stepping aside. "But stop by Balor's office on the way. He asked to see you."

Immediately, my heart sank. In the past couple of hours, I'd been able to push Balor and his smug face to the back of my mind. It had been so very lovely. I'd focused on the mystery at hand and forgot all about the Prince who had forced me into this strange new life. A part of me had kind of hoped that I wouldn't have to come across him again for awhile. It was a big House. There were a lot of fae who lived here. It would be easy to float around without ever having to encounter Balor on a day-to-day basis.

Now, he'd summoned me.

Great.

With a deep breath, I passed through the archway and headed back into the main building of the Court, following Duncan's directions to Balor's office. I spotted a door at the end of the hall. Outside, Moira stood with her head held high, her hand resting lightly on her sword. She spotted me approaching, gave a nod, and relaxed her grip.

"Balor said he was expecting you. Go on in." She smirked as I passed. "And good luck. You're probably going to need it."

Great. That was exactly what I wanted to hear. What the hell was this all about? Surely he hadn't discovered my past in the hours between last night's trial and this afternoon's lunch break. Squaring my shoulders, I pushed the door open and stepped inside.

The first thing I noticed was that Balor looked irritatingly hot sitting behind his oak desk, rich shelves full of books spread out behind him. A single dim lamp with a red shade curved over his desk, illuminating everything in a red sheen. Balor rubbed his sharply cut jaw and motioned to the seat before me. It matched the one he lounged in behind his desk.

"Sit."

"Most people say please when they—"

"I am your Master and your Prince," he said, narrowing his single red eye. "Sit."

Well, okay then. No need to get snippy about it.

Rolling my eyes, I perched on the edge of the seat, still clinging onto the file Elise had given me. "Okay, I'm sitting. What's going on? Duncan said you needed to see me."

"I'm assuming that Elise and Kyle filled you in on what information we have about the missing fae." He scratched his chin. "Tell me what you think about what you learned."

"You're actually asking me for my opinion?" I raised an eyebrow. I was surprised he actually cared. So far, he'd seemed mostly irritated by me and pretty freaking dismissive of my opinion.

"No, I'm telling you to give it to me. And I'm beginning to lose my patience."

Geez. If I'd had any hope of this guy not being a dick once he'd welcomed me into his Court....well, then I'd been dumb as hell. If anything, he'd become even more unbearable.

Of course, he was probably an abductor. Hopefully he wasn't also a murderer, but he might be that, too. So, his attitude wasn't particularly surprising. He probably wanted to know if I suspected him. Like I'd tell him if I did.

And, trust me, *I did*.

"I think that there isn't much to go on yet, and that's kind of concerning." I frowned and tapped the folder with two fingers. " So far, there isn't much evidence. No sign of where they might have been taken, or where they were taken from. Or a motive. Unless you count Fionn, I guess, and I honestly think that might be a stretch. You've had peace for a long time now. I don't know why he'd want to risk that."

Balor pressed his lips into a thin line. "It doesn't sound as though Elise has gone into great detail about our suspicions."

I tapped the folder again. "I think that's why I'm supposed to read this. Over lunch. I haven't eaten yet."

"Telling you will be quicker," he said with a wave of his hand, dismissing both my words and any hope I had of finally getting some damn food into my growling stomach. "I assume you're aware of my policies regarding the other supernatural races."

Ondine had mentioned something in passing once, but I hadn't bothered to stay up-to-date on Balor's political manoeuvrings. I had better things to worry about.

"Why don't you just assume that I know next to nothing."

He gave me a look, and then continued. "Historically, there has always been a lot of mistrust, and flat-out violence, between vampires, shifters, and fae.

We've gone to war on more than one occasion. With our recent shift into the public eye, I've thought it prudent to make alliances with the vampires and shifters of this city. Other Houses are not so keen on this approach."

"Fionn's House you mean," I said with a nod.

"He has been very vocal about his disagreement with me on my policies." Balor placed his hands flat on his desk. "I have warned him, on several occasions, that we should put on a united front, but he continues to exercise his perceived independence from me."

I arched an eyebrow. "Perceived?"

"He is still a part of my Court, despite the long rope I have given him these past few decades. Because of various…reasons…he has more independence than most. But he is still a part of the Crimson Court."

Interesting. Very, very interesting. I filed that info away for later use.

"And so you think he's abducting some of your House members as a way to…disagree with you?" I tried to keep the snark out of my voice, but it was next to impossible. So what if Fionn didn't want to make friends with vampires and shifters? That hardly made him an abductor. Or worse. The word I didn't want to speak aloud: a serial killer.

"I assume you have a better theory," Balor said with a snap.

"There are patterns. Three similar missing girls. When that happens, the culprit tends to be someone who is…disturbed. It doesn't tend to be about politics but about…well, sex." My neck flushed and I glanced away.

"You think this is about sex."

"It definitely could be," I said, glancing back at him. "Think about it. All three of the missing fae are pretty and youthful with brown hair. Maybe someone out there has a twisted fetish for brunettes. Fae brunettes, in particular."

"You're not suggesting the abductor is a human, are you?" Balor said with a snarl. "A human couldn't overpower a fae."

"He could if the fae trusted him or thought him harmless," I said with a shrug. "Or maybe the culprit is another type of supe."

"Now, you're suggesting a vampire or shifter did this." His eye flashed with a kind of darkness that made my toes curl. I couldn't tell if I liked or hated that look on his face, but it definitely affected me, regardless.

I shrugged and tried to smile. "Just saying it's a possibility. That would be the first place I'd look if it were up to me."

"Thankfully, it isn't up to you," he said, leaning back and crossing his arms smugly over his chest. "Because of your initiation into the Court, Fionn is in town. He will be at my club tonight."

"Ooo-kay," I said slowly, not quite getting the point he was trying to make. "Are you hoping to trap him there or something? I doubt he'd nab another girl right there in front of everyone. And don't you need proof? I know you work differently than the human cops, but you still have laws."

"Proof in the form of his thoughts is enough for me," he said with a smile that was more than a tad on the evil end of the smirking spectrum.

Realisation dawned. I should have understood

sooner. He'd made it clear why he'd added me to the investigation team. My mind reading power. He was obviously eager to put it to use. Truthfully? So was I, which kind of pissed me off. I hated feeling like a useful object, but I wanted to find Ondine. Maybe he was just sending me on a wild goose chase, but it was better than sitting on my hands and doing nothing.

It also explained why he didn't want me to tell anyone about my gift. If that info spread to the wrong fae, Fionn would know exactly what I could do. And then he'd know why I'd showed up to the club.

Of course...it was also curious. If Balor was the one behind the missing fae, why would he want to send me to his club to listen in on another Master's thoughts? Maybe as a way to throw me off the scent? One thing I'd learned about Balor was...he wasn't stupid. He probably had a pretty good idea that I suspected him in some capacity. This was a great way to throw me off the scent.

"Alright, so you want me to go and listen to his thoughts," I said. "I'm guessing I should take Moira and Duncan with me? What about Elise and Kyle? I know they're not meant for security, but—"

He waved his hand in dismissal. "You'll go alone."

I blinked at him. "Say what now?"

"No one yet knows what your power is, and I'd like to keep it that way. You'll go alone, and you won't tell anyone what you're doing. Fionn and his warriors have no idea what you look like, thanks to yesterday's glamour." He laced his hands behind his head. "You must not get noticed. Get in, get the information, and then get out without causing any trouble. Tell me you understand."

"I mean, I understand, but—"

"Fionn cannot know that we are investigating him. If so, it could compromise more than just the unsteady peace of my Court." His eye flashed. "If he truly is the one behind this, Ondine's life may be hanging by a thread."

A chill swept down my spine. He was right. If Fionn had abducted Ondine and the others, and he realised that we might be on to him, he might decide that getting rid of them would be the only way to cover up his crimes. And by getting rid of them, I meant...well, you know.

Do some spring cleaning. Feed them to the fishes. Go to the mattresses.

That kind of thing.

And, obviously, that would not be ideal.

If Fionn was even behind this. My sights were still set on Balor, to be honest.

Still, I'd play along and see where it led me. Hell, it was Balor's club, after all. No telling what I might overhear while I was there. The only thing was...

"And you're sure I don't need backup?" I couldn't help but ask.

"If I sent you with backup, you'd get noticed." Balor stood, fiery magic rippling off his powerful body. "Fionn and his team know every single one of my guards. No, you're going to have to do this alone, Clark. Besides, as long as you do what I've told you to do, you won't even need any backup. No one will ever know you were there."

9

"There are a few things you're going to need," Balor said, pressing his hands against his desk to stand tall before me. My eyes dipped to his chest. Even though he wore a jacket, each side draped open to reveal the tighter black shirt beneath. His abs were...well, let's just say that there was no doubting his strength. He could likely throw me across the room if he wanted.

And strangely, that idea didn't terrify me as much as it should...

He caught my glance, smirked, and then slowly buttoned up his jacket as if he had all the time in the world. Every cell in my body felt as if it were on fire. Not from his hidden eye. But from sheer freaking embarrassment. He'd seen me giving him the old eyeball, and his smug self probably thought that meant I wanted to bone him.

And I didn't want to bone him.

Not anything close.

Sure, he was *beyond* fit, but he was a fae Prince.

One who rotated through conquests faster than light. Of course he'd be attractive. He was powerful. He was smart. None of that meant I wanted him.

Because he was also dangerous.

And the enemy.

Definitely *not* the lover.

Of course, he wouldn't want me anyway. Rumor had it Balor liked sweet, smiley, bubbly brunettes. I knew I came off brash and awkward, and my red hair? While I was a fan of the fiery waves, I'd long since learned that most blokes weren't into gingers.

I was the opposite of Balor's type. And I was totally fine with that. *Totally.*

I crossed my arms over my chest and decided to pretend like nothing had happened. There'd been no eyeballing, and he certainly hadn't caught me. "Alright, what do I need?"

"A better outfit, for one." He flicked his eyes across my ensemble and frowned. "That…that will not do."

"Look, mate." I lifted my chin and gestured at my all-black guard ensemble. "Need I remind you that *you're* the one who dressed me in this? It's your own damn uniform. For your own damn guards."

He lifted an eyebrow, his entire body tensing against my words. "Careful, Clark. You're treading far too close to the line again."

Ugh. He was so *annoying*. "I'm not treading close to a line. I am just pointing out the truth. These clothes I'm wearing? You had Moira give them to me."

"Be that as it may," he said. "That outfit is not proper attire for an evening out at my club. Don't think I don't remember what you wore to spy on me."

My cheeks flushed. "You actually remember what I was wearing?"

I wasn't sure I should feel uneasy or kind of complimented by the fact he'd noticed that much about me. It had been a couple of weeks, after all. He saw tons of humans, fae, and otherwise go in and out of his club every week. Sure, I'd been a bit of an anomaly but still. I'd only been wearing a dark pair of trousers and an unassuming blouse. Nothing slinky. Nothing shiny. And still...he remembered.

"Of course I remember. You stuck out like a sore thumb."

I blinked. Lovely. He really was a smooth-talker if there ever was one. Man, if I didn't have to pretend to be subservient to this guy...

"Let me guess," I said. "You're going to have a dress sent up to my room. You do realise that if I kind of suck fighting in my trousers, then I'm definitely going to suck fighting in a dress."

He flashed me a smile full of teeth. "Good thing you won't be doing any fighting then. Listening only, Clark. Keep to yourself and don't cause a stir."

～

Blah, blah, blah. That was all I heard from Balor after that. I kept trying to listen to his mind while he explained the burner phone I was to carry in my handbag and how I was to send him a cryptic text every half hour so that he could be sure I "hadn't gotten up to a load of rubbish" in his club.

It seemed he had a lot of confidence in my ability to handle this mission.

With a heavy sigh, I changed into the tight little red number that he'd had someone deliver to my room. This time, it was far too tight. And far too red. I'd never been what you'd call boobalicious, but somehow, the dress made it seem as though I had some cleavage. It hit just above mid-thigh, which meant that if I bent over, I'd probably flash all of London. With it, I was to wear those same heels I'd been given for my initiation trial.

Great.

The only other thing I was allowed to take with me was my burner phone, which barely fit into the small black clutch that had been sent up with the dress.

A knock sounded on the door just as I was about to head out to the club. For a moment, I frowned at it. Balor had said to keep the details of this mission to myself. And frankly, I didn't want to lie to Moira or Elise or any of the other guards. They'd done nothing but try to help me settle in.

"It's me, Clark. Open up."

A chill swept down my spine, and I wet my lips. I didn't particularly want to see Balor again before I left, partly because he was about to see a whole *hell* of a lot more of me now. The dress was pretty much a bandaid around my middle and nothing more. Not to mention it seriously clashed with my hair. I looked like a clown. A very slutty clown.

"Open up. Now." His voice was firm, insistent.

Swallowing hard, I cracked open the door and peered out. I figured I could pop my face out there and then scramble back inside before he could get the full effect of my outfit. But he pushed hard on the door, and I had to jump out of the way to avoid getting hit. It slammed into the wall with a loud crack.

He strode inside, shoulders thrown back.

Shit. He looked angry. I pressed my sweaty palms against the dress and backed up. There was only one explanation for his sudden anger. He'd figured me out. He knew where I'd come from. It wasn't that big of a leap to make, if he'd taken the time to really think about it. I was an American Courtless fae, one who had been hiding in London. He'd gone and put the pieces of my puzzle together.

He shot out a hand, opened his palm.

"What are you doing?" I asked in a trembling voice. As badass as I wanted to be, my fear had other things on its mind.

"Take this," he said in a rough voice. "I don't think you need it, but it will help you fit in."

I blinked down at his open palm. In it, a tiny black tube covered in glitter sparkled underneath the overhead light in my room. It looked like…

"Is that eyeliner?" I asked incredulously.

Balor Beimnech, bringing me *makeup*? I would laugh if I hadn't just been seconds away from launching myself out of the window in fear.

He shoved the eyeliner into my hands and scowled. "Like I said, you need to fit in, and you're not wearing any. You'll stand out if you go bare-faced like that. Put it on and get going. Remember to text me as soon as you arrive."

He whirled on his feet and disappeared into the hallway without bothering to shut the door behind him. I scowled after him. For a second there, I'd almost let myself believe that he was trying to be nice.

I had to remember not to have that crazy thought again.

The club was just like I remembered. A long line of humans snaked down the side of the building, waiting to pass the red velvet rope that separated the hopefuls from the chosen few. Humans might be wary of us supernaturals, but they sure did like to gawk when they got the chance, and Balor had more than given them that chance.

All were welcome. Fae, vampires, shifters, and humans. The occupants were mostly fae and humans though. Despite the fact that Balor had apparently extended a hand toward the supes of London, they still liked to keep to themselves.

Balor came here once a week. Every Saturday night. It was the busiest time to attend, though the place was still thumping tonight. Even on Thursdays, humans wanted to see those mysterious, immortal creatures whose hundred-year-old skin was every twenty-year-old's dream.

This time, I didn't even have to wait. As I approached the line, the bouncer caught my attention and flicked his fingers for me to cut to the front. With a deep breath, I teetered forward, ignoring the moans and grunts from those stuck waiting for entry. Hell, I could feel the eye daggers being flung into my back. Not a great start for someone who was supposed to stay inconspicuous.

That said, I had to admit the dress had been a perfect choice. Despite feeling as though I couldn't possibly be wearing fewer clothes...many of the humans here tonight were doing just that. Skimpy little numbers that showed off their midriffs, their long legs, and their chiseled collarbones. When I stepped up to the door, I straightened my skirt and stepped inside.

Music pulsed against the walls, and strobe lights swept through the crowd. There were clusters of booths lining one wall while most of the other was consumed by the dance floor. Above it all sat a glass-encased podium where Balor sat every Saturday night to watch the crowd. Only now, Fionn was there instead of my Prince.

Time to get to work.

10

I settled in on a stool near the end of the bar. It kept my hands busy, twirling the ice around in the glass, and I had a great view of the fae inside of the overhead enclosure. There were three of them, all I recognised from the event yesterday. Fionn, and two more whose faces I'd seen in the crowd near the red carpet. A male and a female, both decked out with swords.

They must be part of his army. Fionn's warriors—the Fianna. They were infamous enough that I'd heard of them plenty in my limited access to fae life. They'd been fighting by Fionn's side for centuries, and they were known for their dedication to honour, to Faerie. They even had a saying, three important adages to carry with them always, to stick by no matter what:

Purity of our hearts. Strength of our limbs. Action to match our speech.

It was kind of hard to imagine that one of them would want to abduct some innocents just because they didn't like vampires very much. Didn't sound very pure to me. Or particularly honourable.

"Hi, there." A male fae slid in beside me, decked out in the all-black, sword-wielding ensemble that matched the Fianna above. He had coal black hair, with sharply pointed ears that stuck through the thick strands. His eyes were just as dark as his hair, and his cheekbones were just as sharp as the tips of his ears. He brought with him the scent of grass and snow.

"Oh, hello," I said, straightening on the bar stool. That little movement had the unfortunate side effect of hiking up my already too-short skirt. The male fae's eyes flicked down, but they didn't linger.

"You're fae, but I cannot say I've ever had the pleasure of meeting your acquaintance." His accent was lilting and melodic, and it practically curled off his tongue. If I were a normal girl, I probably would have swooned. Instead, I kind of just gaped at him.

"I'm...er, Marissa," I said, using a name I completely plucked out of thin air. Hey, it would do. I couldn't very well tell him I was Clark, now could I? He was obviously with Fionn, and he'd recognise my actual name from last night's trial.

He arched an eyebrow and slid onto the stool next to mine. "You're American, yes? From the Silver Court?"

Well, I guessed that was my cue to lie through my teeth, since I had done the unthinkable and caught the attention of the wrong fae.

Again.

"Sure," I said, biting my tongue. "I'm here on vacation. Thought I'd come out to Balor's club to see what all the fuss was about."

He let out a moan and placed a hand over his heart. "Please don't tell me you came here hoping to catch Balor's eye. Surely you have better taste than that."

A flicker of irritation went through me. It kind of...annoyed me to hear one of Balor's Court members—even if he was from another House—speaking ill of his Prince. Was that the bond working its magic? It must be. *Ugh.*

"No, if I wanted to catch his eye, I would have come here on a Saturday." I turned to him, gave him a slight smile. "And, as it turns out, there are some more interesting fae here tonight. Are you part of the Fianna?"

"I am." He waved at the bartender, flicking his fingers in some kind of signal. The bartender nodded, whipped out two glasses, and began to make some kind of deep crimson cocktail. "I have been one of Fionn's warriors for a century now."

Damn, this guy was old, but he definitely looked under thirty. Even though I was fae myself and had met plenty of ancient vampires, it still caught me off guard when I came across a fae who was so utterly immortal that it hurt. I mean, this guy's skin was so smooth, my hands begged to reach up and touch his neck.

Ahem.

"I didn't get your name," I said, trying to distract myself from my lurid thoughts and get back on to the task at hand. Maybe if I asked him some questions, I could get some answers.

So, here's the thing about reading minds. Fae are harder to read, though not impossible, except for

Balor. That said, the difficulty level makes it damn near impossible to carry on a conversation while also listening to a mind's thoughts. If I wanted to find out what Fionn, in the glass enclosure above, was thinking? I'd have to sit here very still. My gaze would no doubt go vacant. This guy would know exactly what I was doing. And Balor had made it clear I couldn't let anyone catch on.

Otherwise…well, I didn't really know what he would do. I did know, however, that I didn't want to find out.

"Tiarnan," he said with a smile when the bartender slid the two crimson drinks in front of us. Tiarnan lifted one glass, handed it to me, and lifted the other to his lips. "Cheers. To new beginnings, Marissa."

I cocked my head and clinked my glass against his, but then turned my mind onto his thoughts.

I think she's given me a fake name, but I don't blame her. She's here alone in a strange city. In a strange Court. I hope I'm not making her nervous.

Huh. That was…nicer than I expected. And certainly not as leery. I won't go into detail about the kind of thoughts I'd overheard from guys chatting me up, but let's just say there was a lot more focus on boobs and bums.

"So, what are you doing in town?" I asked, arching a brow. "I'm obviously not from around here, but neither are you."

Can't tell her about my upcoming trip to the West Norwood catacombs at midnight tomorrow. Tell her about something else. Oh, the trial. There we go.

"The Crimson Court initiated a new fae yesterday.

As you know, all Masters must be present at the trial." He scowled. "Unfortunately, she ended up staying in Balor's House. Truly a shame. That's just one more fae who will side with his ridiculous notion that we can befriend the vampires."

Balor and his alliances. Someone needs to stop him before it gets worse.

That strange irritation sparked to life from deep within me, making my face burn. It felt next to impossible to keep my hands to myself. My blood roared in my veins, and a voice awoke inside of me. One that drowned out everything else.

It wanted revenge. It wanted Tiarnan to pay. It hated the words it had heard from his mouth, from his mind.

It made me take my glass away from my lips and tip it right over Tiarnan's head.

"Oh my god," I whispered the second the red liquid ran down his face. The crimson drink covered everything. His dark hair, that sharp jawline, those cheeks. Horror chased away the anger, and all my blood drained from my face. That burning sensation? Totally gone. Now I felt nothing but the cold hard truth of reality.

I had just poured a drink over Tiarnan's head.

Tiarnan sat frozen on his stool, the bright red liquid dripping into his mouth. He raised his gaze, his dark eyes hardening on my horror-stricken face. "I knew it was too good to be true. A beautiful female fae, visiting from the states. But you're one of *his*."

"I really am sorry. I don't know what came over me," I said in a rush of words. Truth was, I actually was sorry. This guy had been pretty nice to me so far, and while the whole catacombs thing had piqued some interest, his thoughts were not those of some kind of crazy serial killer.

"I'll tell you what came over you." He carefully set his half-empty glass on the bar, stood from the stool, and wiped the drink from his chin. "Your bond with your Master kicked in, *Clark*. You're obviously new or you would have understood what was happening, and you would have been able to control yourself a bit more. Enjoy your evening."

Yep, well. So, I'd definitely made a wrong turn here. Not only had I chased away a good looking, decent guy, I'd also made a scene and revealed the fact that I was the newbie fae in Balor's Court, the one who had her trial the previous night.

Whoops.

It was probably time I got out of here. Sure, I'd have to slink out with my tail between my legs, but I couldn't risk still being around when Tiarnan no doubt went up to his own Master to tell him what had happened. At least I hadn't given away my whole mind-reading thing.

Now, *that* would have been a disaster.

"Well, look what we have here." A female fae with short spiky hair shoved in front of me when I attempted to make a swift exit toward the door. She stood before me, arms crossed, eyebrows raised. Oh yeah. And she was also carrying a freaking sword.

"Excuse me," I said. "You're in my way."

A male fae, boxy and built like a tank, stood beside her. Together, they made a wall between the bar and the door. This guy looked a lot like Duncan, only his bare arms were covered in half-finished tattoos, almost like he decided half-way through that he no longer wanted them.

"We overheard your conversation with Tiarnan," the male said with a laugh. "We don't have a lot of time for vampire lovers."

"Look. I didn't ask to be initiated into Balor's House, okay?" I held up my hands and shrugged. "That's where Caer placed me, so that's where I ended up. Can I go now?"

The female snorted. "Damn, you really are new. Don't you know why fae get placed in certain Houses? Because Caer can read your soul. She knew you would belong with him. That means you'll be a hell of a lot like him."

"I am nothing like Balor Beimnech."

"Careful." The female gave me a glittering smile. "If you talk too much shite about your Master, you'll end up pouring a drink over your own head."

Spiky Hair and Tattoo Dude obviously found the whole thing much more hilarious than I did. They both burst out laughing, high-fiving each other like they were at some kind of sporting event. And I was definitely on the losing team.

"Yeah, yeah," I said, holding up my hands. "You got me. Now, move, before I have to call my Master and tell him you're being wankers. Don't forget. He's your Prince, too."

Spiky Hair's eyebrow winged toward her hairline, and she glanced at her pal with the tattoos. "You hear that, Bear? She thinks we're being wankers."

"Maybe we should show her what a wanker really looks like," he answered with a grin.

Before I knew what was happening, both Spiky

Hair and Tattoo Dude had thrown their bodies into what I imagined was their Fight Mode. They were bouncing on the balls of their feet, fists raised, eyes narrowed. They'd look kind of ridiculous, bopping around like they were dancing to the beat of the music, if they weren't also directing that hostile energy toward me.

Thing was, I knew I was in way over my head, but I couldn't very well turn tail and run. I might be a lot of things, but a coward wasn't one of them.

"Fine." I sighed and tried to match their stance.

But before I could get into position, a fist hurtled right toward my face. Tattoo Guy's knuckles made contact. Pain lanced through my cheek. And, I hate to admit it, I landed flat on my back. I groaned and blinked up at the ceiling, bright stars melting into the strobe lights that pulsed through the cavernous space.

Someone grabbed me, and I got hauled to my feet. It took me a moment to realise it was the bouncer from the door and that he was now dragging me through the crowd. A crowd full of curious faces. I'd been tasked with doing anything but causing a scene, and I'd done the total opposite.

Balor was going to kill me.

Just as we reached the door, I took one risky glance over my shoulder. Tiarnan and Fionn stood side by side against the glass wall, staring down at me. They wore matching frowns, and then Tiarnan whispered something into Fionn's ear. My mind reached out toward them, desperate to hear what they were thinking—

"Ow!"

The bouncer hurled me onto the ground outside and glared down at me. I rubbed my elbow, scowling.

"Was that really necessary? *He* punched *me*."

"Balor told me to keep an eye on you, and kick you the hell out of here if you caused trouble. Doesn't matter who started it. That was trouble. And your Master is not going to be pleased."

11

As I dragged myself back to the Court, it didn't escape my notice that this was a perfect opportunity for me to get the hell out of here. No one was watching me, which meant no one could stop me. Balor probably wouldn't realise I'd fled until I was outside of the city. I could run. I could flee. Leaving the Court could happen sooner than I'd thought possible.

That said…I couldn't. Not yet. I was no closer to finding Ondine or discovering what had happened to the other missing fae. I'd made a promise to myself. And to my friend. I would stay long enough for me to find her, and then I'd save myself. I couldn't go back on my word, even if a storm in the form of Balor Beimnech was headed my way.

So, I went back to my new home, sucked in a deep breath, and stepped through the door. Balor stood in the sparkling, chandelier-lit entryway, his entire body practically trembling with anger. He hooked a finger at me, spun on his heels, and stormed down the hallway toward his office. I followed behind without a single word, blood rushing through my ears. This was going to be bad.

Why hadn't I fled again? I probably should have fled.

"Sit," Balor said when we reached his office, after he'd shut the door behind us. He spoke in a surprisingly calm voice, and his eye wasn't yet blazing with anger. The only thing that gave away his true emotions was the way he stood tensely behind his desk, one hand braced on the wood and the other tucked behind his back.

I sat.

"Fionn has informed me that you were at my club tonight, dumping drinks on his Fianna and provoking fights," he said in a dangerously low voice. "Elaborate."

"Let me just start by saying that while what he told you is technically true, it is also kind of misleading," I said, wetting my lips. "I didn't start the fight. I was on my way to leave the club when I got cornered by Spiky Hair and Tattoo Guy."

His lips quirked. "Riawna and Bear. Continue."

I rolled my eyes. Even in a situation like this, he felt the need to correct me. "Fine. Riawna and Bear. They blocked me from leaving, started taunting me, and then Bear punched me."

"Fionn informed me that you called them wankers," he said, voice still low and dangerous enough to cause a sliver of ice to slide down my spine. I had kind of hoped we could avoid the whole wanker business.

"Er. Okay, so I maybe called them wankers, but—"

"Clark," he growled.

"Look. Don't blame me." I held up my hands, scooting back in my chair to put some space between us. His growl was making me two parts scared and one part kind of turned on, and I didn't like either of those emotions. This bond thing was really starting to piss me off. "You didn't tell me the bond would make me act like some kind of hormonal defender of your name."

His eye softened, just a bit. "You're honestly telling me that the bond made you call the Fianna wankers?"

"Yeah, kind of." I fiddled with the edge of the red dress. "They were going on about you being a vampire lover and laughing at me for ending up in your House, so…"

"Okay, I'll accept that as an explanation, even if I don't approve," Balor said. "Now, why did you dump the drink over Tiarnan's head?"

"The same reason," I said. "At first, I let him think I was from the Silver Court—"

"Good thinking," he murmured, and I felt a thrill go down my spine.

"So then he brought up the trial last night, saying it was a shame the new fae got initiated into your Court. Because of your vampire obsession or something. He only said a few harmless things, but it was like my blood was boiling. And then my hand just did whatever it wanted."

"The bond made you want to defend me." His voice was measured, even. I couldn't tell if I'd managed to soften his anger, or if I'd only made it worse. "It's been a long time since I initiated a Courtless fae into my House. I thought it would take longer for your bond to kick in so strongly. While your actions were less than ideal, I cannot help but appreciate your motives."

My heart did a little flutter in my chest, but I put a scowl on my face to mask it. "Don't get all soft or whatever. I didn't do it on purpose."

He frowned and stomped toward me, fire now dancing in his single red eye. I sucked in a breath and scooted back in the chair, a new thrill of fear and excitement storming through me. I didn't quite understand it, this effect he had on me. I knew it was because of the bond, but it was still weird as hell.

Still, I felt it, whatever it was. So much that I had to grip the arms of the chair.

"You have put this whole Court in jeopardy. You have not only offended one of Fionn's most respected Fianna, but you have provoked a fight with two others. It has been years since our Houses have exchanged blows. Tensions were high before, but they will be even worse now."

"But don't you suspect Fionn of abducting Ondine and the others?"

He released the tension from his shoulders and turned toward the window, his muscular frame now a silhouette against the early morning sky. "I do. Tell me what you learned."

I bit my lip and thought back to the words I heard echoing in Tiarnan's mind. Something about a trip to the catacombs, but nothing more than that. Nothing concrete, and nothing really to suggest that Fionn had a damn thing to do with the abductions. I should probably tell Balor about the catacombs, but the thing was…I still didn't trust him, especially not when he was storming around his office like an angel of death.

"I didn't learn anything useful. Your bouncer kicked me out before I could get into Fionn's mind."

He whirled toward me. "You're telling me that you got yourself kicked out of my club before you could get some useful information."

My cheeks flamed. "I didn't really have much time."

He let out a weary sigh before easing around his desk and sinking into the leather chair. Closing his eye, he ran a hand down his face, suddenly looking very tired. For the first time, I felt a twinge of sympathy for this Prince. He almost seemed like he cared, like he was concerned for his missing fae.

Of course, it might be nothing more than an act.

"I never thought things would get to this point again," he muttered to himself. "History is repeating itself, and I cannot bear to do now what I did then."

I leaned forward. "What are you talking about?"

He glanced up sharply then, as if he were surprised that I'd heard him. His eye narrowed, and his palms hit the top of his desk hard. "Get out of my head."

I blinked at him, confused, but then it all became clear. Balor wasn't as impenetrable as I'd first thought. He'd let some thoughts slip, when he wasn't paying attention to himself. Thoughts that I had to admit had more than piqued my curiosity. What history was repeating itself? And what had he done?

"I actually wasn't trying to listen. Your thoughts slipped out." I waited a moment before letting my curiosity get the better of me. "There's a lot I don't know about this world. It's better if I understand it. What history were you thinking about?"

"None of your concern." Balor stood and crossed the room to the door before opening it wide. He ushered me out with a newfound coldness in his eye. "Return to your quarters and get some rest. Tomorrow will be a busy day since you were unable to fulfil your duty tonight."

I barely even noticed the insult. Instead, I was far too focused on the sudden shift in his temperament. Looked like I wasn't the only one who was trying to hide her past. Balor Beimnech was carrying a secret.

And I was going to be the one to figure it out.

12

A knock sounded on my door, and I groaned. After my little adventure at Balor's club, I'd decided to slink up to my room, change into PJs, and huddle underneath the blankets until morning. I just wanted to hide from the world for awhile. Unfortunately, Moira and Elise had a different plan in mind. They barged through the door without waiting for me to open it and plopped onto the bed.

"Hi?" I raised my eyebrows. Neither of them were wearing their guard uniforms. Instead, they were decked out in PJs much like mine, soft fleece covered in little animals. It made them seem…I don't know, more human than fae, even with their pointed ears and criminally-smooth hair. Kind of a relief after the day I'd had.

"Rumor has it Balor sent you on a secret mission to his club," Elise said, her silver eyes shining like twin full moons.

"And rumor has it you pissed off the Fianna and got kicked out." Moira looked a little less amused but just as curious. She tucked a golden strand of hair behind her ear and leaned closer. "We need details."

"Well, the rumors are true."

Balor hadn't exactly told me it was safe to share what I'd been up to tonight, but if word had already started to spread? I couldn't exactly lie. It would be easy enough to prove that I'd been there. Crimson Court fae had likely been in attendance, and they would have seen what had gone down.

The drink dumping. The wanker calling.

"Tell us everything," Elise said as she pulled a bar of chocolate from her pocket. She bit off a chunk before asking, "Is Balor super angry?"

"Ahhh...yes." I greedily took a square of chocolate when she passed it to me. "Balor sent me to his club to do some recon for our case. He wanted me to see what I could find out since none of the House Futrail fae knew what I looked like, thanks to the whole glamouring thing from the trial. Unfortunately...things didn't go according to plan."

"That makes sense," Moira said with a nod. "I never would have thought to send you, but Balor was right. Easy for you to get in and out without being noticed. Great opportunity to weasel out some information." She pressed her lips together, biting back a smile. "If you had managed to keep yourself from dumping a drink over Tiarnan's head, of course."

Elise snorted, and then covered her mouth. "I can't believe you did that."

"Honestly?" I chewed on another chunk of chocolate and hugged my pillow to my chest. "Neither can I. It's like this fire took over my body, and I had no control over my actions. It just happened. And there was nothing I could do to stop it."

Moira nodded emphatically. "It's the bond. You're new to it, so it's all really raw. You'll get better at controlling your actions over time, but you'll never fully be able to push away the feelings it causes. It's really easy to get worked up when that magic springs to life."

"Yeah, but have you ever dumped a drink over a guy's head because of it?"

She grinned. "No, Clark. I can't say I have."

"Eh, don't worry about it, lovely. Tiarnan is right up Fionn's bum," Elise said. "He probably deserved it."

For the first time since I'd arrived at the Court, I had to laugh, a little at least. Partly at myself. Partly at the ridiculousness of my situation. And partly at the chocolate smeared across Elise's cheek. I felt more relaxed than I had in a long time. Like I was almost part of something, and these two females were right there in the thick of it with me.

"Thanks, girls. You aren't…I don't know, mad at me?"

Confusion rippled across Elise's face. "Why would we be mad at you?"

"Well, for one, I'm part of your team now, and I didn't tell you what I was up to," I said. "And two, I screwed up my first mission. In a bad way."

"Everyone cocks up sometimes," Elise said. "Besides, your bond kicked in. I could hardly blame you for that."

"And not telling us? You were only acting on Balor's orders," Moira added. "I imagine he didn't want word to spread that you were going to be at the club tonight. I'd be more angry if you'd told us when he explicitly asked you not to."

Right. Because service and loyalty to the Master was the most important to them. Above all else.

Speaking of our Master…

"So…" I couldn't believe I was about to ask this question, but I reminded myself that it was for a good cause. For Ondine. For Rosalind and Abby, the other two missing fae. For the Court. "What's Balor like? Is he really as bad as his reputation?"

Elise smirked, leaned back against the pillows, and passed me the rest of the chocolate. "Ah, there it is. I was wondering how long it would take you to ask about his sex life. You fancy him."

Heat filled my neck. "What are you talking about? I'm just trying to understand my Master."

"Right." Moira chuckled. "You and every other single female in this House. Trust me. We've seen it before. We might not get newbies around here often, but we do get visitors. Everyone wants to know about Balor and his reputation. How often he has sex. What kind of females he's into. We've heard it all before, Clark. *Many* times."

"I swear, I am not interested in him. I just want to know more about him." Still, the heat stayed in my neck, flushing further up into my cheeks. I cleared my throat. "I'm new. Humour me a bit. So…what's he like?"

"Ah." Moira's grin died. "I'm afraid the stories are true. He's a womaniser, and he pulls a different bird every week. Every Saturday night at his club. Always someone he's never met before, and never someone from his own Court. That said, he's picky about taking it any further than that."

"Picky?" I arched an eyebrow. "Picky how?"

"We've never actually seen him bring any girls back to the House," Elise said with a shrug. "Not that it means he hasn't. There are secret doorways here that no one knows about but him. That said…we're his guards. Someone is on shift at all times. If he brought a girl back here, we would probably know about it."

Secret doorways? How…interesting.

I poked a bit into Elise's mind, only enough to get a fleeting thought. She was much easier to read than Moira, but I didn't want to pry too much. I was still trying to carry on a conversation with the both of them, and I couldn't risk going weirdly vacant. Plus…I didn't really want to spy on their minds. They'd been nothing but nice to me.

Hope she doesn't fancy him too much. He'll only end up breaking her heart.

It took all my self-control not to scowl.

Balor Beimnech, breaking *my* heart? Yeah, good luck with that, mate.

"Here." Elise dug into her bag and pulled out a small round object wrapped in brown paper. Instantly, the scent of cinnamon wafted through the room. My stomach grumbled. In all the excitement, I'd forgotten to have anything for dinner. The chocolate had been great and all, but that wasn't nearly enough food to satisfy my shifter hunger.

I opened the package and found a small, very delicious looking cake topped with gooey frosting. "What's this?"

"Call it a commiseration gift," Moira said. "I know it's not fun to get chewed out by the boss."

"We're by your side," Elise quickly added. "You're one of us now, and we've got your back."

Smiling, I bit into the gooey cake. Deep down, I couldn't help but feel a twinge of guilt. These two fae, Moira and Elise, had welcomed me into their fold. And all I wanted to do was get the hell out. Would they still have my back if they knew the truth?

I didn't think so. And that made me sadder than I wanted to admit. But hey, at least I had some cake.

∼

Despite the early wake-up call I'd had that morning, and despite the very eventful evening at Balor's club, I couldn't sleep. My mind was far too active, and I still had tubs of adrenaline pouring through my veins. I tried counting sheep. And then I tried counting vampires. Hell, I even tried counting Balor faces bopping up and down on his club's dance floor.

None of it worked. In fact, the Balor face bopping only woke me up even more. My body hummed with the need to do something, anything. I needed to get active. Go for a run or find a punching bag. The tension thrumming through me made me feel as if I were about to explode, and I needed to find some kind of release or I wouldn't sleep for a month.

So, I did what any other warm-blooded female fae would do in this situation. I slid a jumper over my head and decided to spy on my Master.

His unspoken words had lit a million questions in

my mind. Not to mention that I was more than aware of the ticking clock when it came to Ondine. She'd been missing almost forty-eight hours now. We didn't have long. While I'd let down my guard, far more than I'd wanted due to that damn bond, I needed to keep my eye on the prize.

I needed to start investigating Balor.

I pushed out into the hallway. Dim lights were held in sconces along the walls, and every door was shut tight. All the fae had gone to bed hours ago, which meant I pretty much had run of the place.

That said, I wasn't dumb enough to believe that I could do anything I wanted without being seen. There were cameras strategically placed throughout the property, and there would be one guard on rotation, just in case an enemy tried to breach the front gates.

Luckily, I'd had plenty of time rolling around in my bed to come up with an excuse for my nighttime excursion. And it was pretty close to the truth.

I hadn't been able to sleep. I'd been too wired from my first day at Court. So, I thought I'd take a look around my new home. A kind of self-hosted tour of the property.

There was no reason for anyone to suspect that I was up to anything fishy.

I tiptoed along the hallway, keeping my eyes peeled for any sign of cameras in the corners. I passed two with their little blinking lights, but no alarm sounded in response. When I reached the stairs, I thought about sneaking toward Balor's office. But...maybe there would be something more interesting to find in his bedroom.

Of course, I didn't know where that was. But if I

was a betting kind of girl? I would put a hundred quid on the very top of the building. He probably had a penthouse with a perfect view of the city's skyline.

With a deep breath, I went up.

And I was rewarded for my efforts. At the very top of the curving staircase sat a single door flanked by two massive potted trees. It was made of solid wood, and it had a metal plaque engraved with the crest of the Beimnech family. A dragon with fire streaming out of its open mouth.

Bingo. I'd found Balor's 'flat' so to speak. Now, I had to do something about getting inside.

Just as I was one millisecond away from wrapping my trembling hand around the doorknob and giving it a good twist, the knob moved out of its own volition. So, I reacted in a completely normal fashion by muffling a shriek and throwing myself behind one of the trees.

The door drifted open, and Balor's voice reached out to me. He stepped into the hallway, frowning as he spoke urgently into a cell phone pressed tightly against his ear.

He was dressed in a dark, fitted suit that hugged every muscle in his body—and he had a shed load of muscles. I wet my lips as I watched him run his fingers through his hair. He mussed up the brown-and-silver strands in a way that made him appear even more delicious than he usually did. If that was even possible. His body hummed with power, with the unmistakable electricity that only a ruler would have. There was a reason he was the one in charge and not someone else.

He was terrifying and magnetic all at once.

"So, you have never heard of a fae by the name of

Clark." He shook his head and frowned. "There must be some record of her. She can't have just appeared out of thin air."

A chill swept down my spine. Here I was, trying to find out Balor's secret. And he was trying to find out mine. Who was he talking to? What information had he gotten? From the sound of it, not much.

Yet.

"No, she doesn't seem to know either." Balor loosed a breath. "Yes, I know she could be lying, but what would be the point?" Another pause. "Okay, ring me when you have more information."

Balor sighed and slid his phone into his pocket. He locked his door behind him, and then disappeared down the carpeted stairs. All the while, I stood hidden behind the tree, my heart hammering so hard that my ribs hurt. Someone Balor knew was looking into my past. If they dug deep enough, they might be able to track down the truth. My grandmother had done everything she could to bury it, but she hadn't counted on the Prince of the Crimson Court to come looking for me.

With a deep breath, I took one last look at his door and decided not to push my luck. If he caught me in there, his suspicions would only get worse. I'd have to investigate him some other way.

13

After my little lurking expedition around the Court, I still had a hard time falling asleep. Might've had something to do with the phone call I'd overheard. You know, the fact that my life was practically hanging in the balance while Balor's contact dug deep into my past to find out where I'd come from.

Plus, I wasn't any closer to finding out if Balor had something to do with the disappearances. No lead on where Ondine was. No answers. Just questions.

I probably passed out around three o'clock. And then a fist slammed on my door at six. Again.

Blurry-eyed, I threw back my covers, shuffled across the room, and opened the door. Only this time, there was no Moira.

It was Balor. All bright-eyed and bushy-tailed. He looked annoyingly good for six o'clock in the morning. Dark leather jacket with trousers that were clearly tailored. It was criminal how well they fit his impossibly-strong legs. His dark hair was expertly ruffled, the silver strands peeking through. Even his eye patch fit perfectly. Of course, I was pretty sure it was impossible for him to look terrible. Unlike me.

He frowned at my hair, now doubling as a bush. "Why do you look like that?"

I'm pretty sure that was the first time Balor had ever asked me a full question, and what a pleasant one at that.

"I didn't get much sleep," I said, absently patting down my crazed bed hair. There'd been no time to wash it yesterday, so it was even more of a disaster than usual.

Why was he even *here*? Couldn't he leave me alone for more than two seconds? Was he checking up on me? Ensuring that I hadn't vanished in the middle of the night?

"Well, get dressed." He threw some clothes at me —also black, just like all of the others I'd been given. "The guards are having a meeting at eight, so we don't have much time."

My eyebrows winged upward. "Time for what?"

His eye flicked up and down my body, and I couldn't help but blush underneath his scrutinising gaze. "You're an enigma, Clark, but there is one thing I'm certain of when it comes to you. Your fighting skills are nonexistent. It's time for you to train."

~

When I padded into the sparring room with Balor, I expected to find someone like Duncan or Moira there to take me through the motions of what it meant to be a guard for House Beimnech. Instead, the lofted space was chillingly empty.

Beams criss-crossed overhead, and our footsteps echoed as we moved off the stone and onto the padded floor. Weapons had been hung up along a far wall, steel glinting against the dim sconce lighting. There were no windows. No exit but the one.

Balor peeled off his jacket and dropped it on the padded floor. He was wearing a tight-fitted tank and dark trousers. I wet my lips. He looked good, damn him. Too good. So good that his muscles were going to be a distraction. Also? I knew I was toast. He could knock me flat on my ass, regardless of whether I'd had any training or not.

With a twitch of his lips, he jerked his chin toward the wall where several swords were hanging from golden hooks. "Eventually, I would like to get you to the point where you can carry one of those for protection. I've reserved the one on the far right just for you."

My heart twitched. "Seriously?"

He got me a sword? That was, strangely, one of the nicest things anyone had ever done for me. It made me feel...kind of special.

"Every guard gets a sword, even the ones on the investigation team. Elise and Kyle have them, too."

"Oh. Right." So, maybe not so special then. "That's cool, but I've got to be honest. I'm a little worried that the sword would end up hurting me far more than it would end up hurting a potential enemy."

He shot me a smile full of teeth. "That is why we're not starting you out with the sword. We'll use our bodies only."

Bodies only.

A shiver went down my spine, and a delicious heat curled in my gut. There was something so suggestive in the way he'd said those words. Or was there? I couldn't tell if he was being provocative or if my stupid overactive hormones were making my brain melt.

That was it. I knew what Balor's powers were now. His magic was the sole reason that he was so good with the ladies. He could cast an allure, a spell that could make anyone swoon. That had to be it and nothing more. And he was doing it to me now.

It had nothing to do with his impossibly good looks. Or with the way his eye seemed to look inside my soul and see everything. Or the way he spoke, his deep, dark voice slithering across my skin. Or his woody, heady scent of oak, moss, and danger.

I wet my lips again. I needed to focus.

"I feel like this probably isn't an even playing field." I watched him stalk from one end of the padded floor to the other. "You're the Master of this House. And a Prince. I'm totally new here, and I've never been trained."

"You're right."

He stopped pacing and closed the distance between us. I had to drop back my head to look up at him. It was the first time I'd truly realised just how tall he really was. Over six feet, most definitely. Combined with that raw power that rippled off of him? It was all

I could do not to trip on my feet and fall flat on my ass. Just from looking at him.

"So, are you going to go get someone else to train me?" My voice came out a whisper.

"Most definitely not," he said. "You need to be prepared to face off against the most powerful enemies out there. Whether or not you realise it, you're a target now. If Fionn is the one behind these abductions, he could come for you next. And, if our time of peace comes to an end, you're going to need to be able to fight. Not only to protect this Court but to keep yourself alive."

Chills swept down my spine. I hadn't really thought about it like that, but he was right. Last night, I'd brazenly waltzed in front of a potential enemy, one whose eyebrows I must have raised. He wouldn't have to be a genius to figure out I'd been there to investigate him or his Fianna, especially if he knew I'd joined Balor's guard team.

I didn't fit the profile of the missing girls, but that didn't mean anything if he thought I was on to him.

Suddenly, I felt impossibly helpless.

And I *refused* to stay that way.

"Alright." I sucked a deep breath into my lungs and squared my shoulders. "I see your point. I'm in. Show me what you've got."

"Good." He flashed me that eerie, unnerving smile of his. "Because it wasn't a question. It was an order, Clark."

I tried not to show my irritation at his words. I really, really didn't like being ordered around, but I was also playing a role here. The dutiful fae, obeying her Master's every command. *Ugh.* The words grated on my nerves.

Plus, I really did need to learn how to fight.

Anyway, that was about the time that everything went sideways. And I do mean literally sideways. Somehow, before I even knew what was happening, the thick blue mats rose up to meet my face. My breath got knocked from my lungs, and stars danced in my eyes. With a growl, I rolled onto my back to glare up at Balor's smirking face.

He looked far too pleased with himself.

"I thought you were going to train me. Not knock me senseless."

He held out a hand, eye still sparkling. "I *am* going to train you. That was just a demonstration of the first move you're going to learn. No punching. No kicking. We need to start with a basic move that will allow you to flee if you get into a sticky situation. And that can be accomplished by simply flattening your opponent on the floor."

I pushed up from the floor and propped my fists on my hips. "I think you probably could have explained that without demonstrating it first."

"Maybe so," he said smoothly as he edged around to my left side. "But I am a strong proponent of first-hand experience."

Interesting. Another little factoid about Balor to file away.

"Now," he said, reaching out to brush his hand along my waist. I stiffened, heart racing. Despite the fact that I still *kind of* (half-heartedly) suspected him of abducting his own Court members, my body rebelled against me. A very deep and dangerous part of me wanted to shift closer, to feel more of his warm hand along my body. His allure was so strong that one stupid, simple touch practically made my head spin.

"You'll need to brace yourself," he murmured, taking a small step closer. His power rippled across my skin. Strands of silky magic caressed my neck. "You will only have seconds to make your move. You need to be fast. You need to be purposeful. Any hesitation could cost you."

His chest brushed against mine. My mouth went dry. What were we talking about again? Something about hesitation.

Hell, I didn't feel any hesitation.

"Careful," he murmured before leaning down to sniff along my neck. Yes, he actually sniffed me. The wild thing was, I didn't push him away. Instead, I closed my eyes and tilted back my head so that he could have better access to my thrumming skin. "Your adrenaline is spiking, and I can smell it."

My eyes flew open. "You can smell it?"

"Oh yes." He smiled and dragged his nose across the base of my neck again. I shuddered in response, every cell on my body desperately in need of more. "It is my power. I can smell far more than you expect. Including the fact that you're hiding something from me."

He stepped back then, leaving me practically gasping for more. My heart panicked as it lurched around my chest, and my palms were so sweaty that even rubbing them against my shirt didn't help.

I didn't understand what had come over me. One

minute, I'd been ready to fight. The next, I'd been practically purring from his touch. And the jackass looked smug as hell about it, even while his red eye flashed.

So, he could smell the fact I was hiding something from him.

That...was unsettling.

"I don't understand how you could smell something like that." I pressed my hair away from my face, trying to block out the desire he'd made me feel. "You're lying."

"I am not lying." His voice dropped into a growl. "What are you hiding from me, Clark? What is it that you do not want me to know?"

I gritted my teeth and glanced away. "Nothing."

"I order you to tell me." He stepped forward and grasped my face in his strong hand. "I am your Master and your Prince."

Closing my eyes, I tried not to give in to the allure of his touch again. "So you've said. I'm to follow you like the good little puppy dog I am."

"That wasn't what I was going to say," he said in a firm voice. "I was going to say that you should let yourself trust me. You're now part of my Court and my House. Therefore, you're my responsibility now, just like every other fae who lives here."

"Just like Ondine? And Rosalind, and Abby?" I asked, flipping my eyes open to catch the look on his face when I said their names.

He flinched and dropped his hand from my cheek. "That was a low blow, Clark. I am doing everything I can to find them, and you know it, including adding a mind reader to the investigation team. One who *refuses* to trust me."

"Speaking of mind reading," I said, newly bolstered. "I am clearly not the only one in this room who isn't being totally open. You won't let me read your mind."

"Of course I won't," he said in a snap. "There are far too many things that are dangerous for you to know. No one reads my mind, and that certainly includes a fae who lives inside my own damn House."

Anger rippled off his body in waves. His jaw tightened as he ground his teeth together. For a moment, I thought he would storm out of the sparring room, leaving me here to figure out how to protect myself all on my own.

But then he turned back toward me. "Enough of this. You *will* tell me what you're hiding, but it does not have to be today. Now, bend your knees. Chest up. Shoulders back."

I did as he said. He made a few corrections. Chest up a bit more. Stance a bit more bouncy and make sure I put my weight in the middle of my foot. I felt kind of ridiculous standing there with my boobs pressed out as far as they could go, but Balor seemed satisfied.

"Keep your core tight and hold your breath."

I did as he said.

He gave a nod and suddenly shoved his hand against my shoulder. Surprisingly, I didn't fall flat on my face. Instead, I…well, I stayed in place.

"Good." He gave a nod and moved around me in a circle. "I want you to practice this stance as much as possible in your free time until it becomes second nature. Now, hold your breath again."

He shoved hard against both shoulders this time, but I gritted my teeth, kept my core tight, and managed to stay on my feet. Balor smiled, and I couldn't help but grin right back.

"Good. You're catching on fast. Now let's see if you can knock your Prince off his feet."

14

Knocking Balor onto the floor was…not as easy as the whole core tightening thing. In fact, it was damn near impossible. I was pretty much half his size, and my strength was barely even a quarter, if that. He showed me over and over again how to crouch and hurl my legs in a circle. The aim was to sweep the opponent right off his feet.

All I managed to do was add a plethora of bruises to my shin.

Breath heaving, I glared at him. He was like a rock, immovable, and hard as hell. And his so-called training didn't seem to be doing anything other than making me worse. Instead of flailing around on the ground, I needed to learn how to actually hit something. Preferably with something pointy.

"That's enough for today." He brushed off his shirt as though *he* were the one who had landed, repeatedly, on the padded floor. "You need to be at the team meeting in fifteen minutes."

"Fifteen minutes?!" That meant that almost two

hours had flown by. I'd gotten so wrapped up in training that I'd barely even noticed the time. It felt like seconds ago that we'd walked into the sparring room. And strangely, all my anger and fear had been forgotten.

For a little while, at least.

"I don't know what you're waiting for, Clark." Balor took a large step back and shuttered his emotions. "You're already on thin ice after your performance yesterday evening. Don't make it worse by being late."

~

I actually was late. Two minutes in fact. I'd stormed up the stairs and changed into my guard uniform, patting some water onto my face and into my armpits. Gross, I know, but I didn't have any other choice.

Moira bit back a grin when I sauntered into the command station but Balor didn't share her amusement. Even though he was the idiot who caused me to be late in the first place. Also? How did he look so damn good when we'd both rushed out of the sparring room at the same damn time? Somehow, he was pristine and completely unruffled. Unlike me.

"You're late," he said crisply. "I'm unsure of your punishment, but you will have one."

I just gaped at him.

"Right. Duncan. Tell us what we have," Balor continued, turning back to the leader of the guard team.

Duncan shuffled some papers and frowned.

"Unfortunately, not much. It's now been over forty-eight hours since Ondine went missing. We have no evidence pointing at anyone. Lesley has spoken to every single fae in this House. None of them saw anything the night she disappeared."

Lesley held up a hand and gave a strangely weak smile. Out of all of the guards, I'd spoken to her the least. She was always busy with her duties, rarely in the command station. Now I understood why. She'd been canvassing the entire House for info. It irritated me a little bit that Balor hadn't considered me for the job. My powers would have proved useful in that situation. Instead, he'd sent me out in a party dress to make a fool of myself.

"From what I've gathered," she said in a soft voice, "Ondine went to her room around nine and never came out. She doesn't show up on the security cameras at any point after that. But her room is on the third floor, and her window was intact."

That was really freaking strange.

"Of course, maybe she doesn't show up on the tapes because she was glamoured," Lesley said, shooting a strange eyeball toward Elise. Elise merely sniffed in response.

Glamoured. I supposed that made sense. Ondine could have gone into her room, been glamoured by a fae, and then been taken out that way.

Out of curiosity, I quickly reached out toward my new friend's mind. I didn't want to suspect her, but…I couldn't help but wonder…

How dare Lesley passive aggressively accuse me of taking Ondine. I wouldn't hurt a fly, and she knows it. Hell, I'm vegan.

Inwardly, I sighed in relief and returned my attention to the conversation at hand. Elise wasn't behind the abductions. I shouldn't have even doubted her, but every single fae was a suspect at this point. Hell, I wouldn't even blame them for suspecting me.

"Last night, our mission to get evidence on Fionn's potential involvement backfired." Balor shot me a weighted glance. "But we need to make another attempt. If he truly is the one behind the disappearances, and it looks like he is, his movements should give him away. I'm going to put two of you on him tonight. Follow him, track his comings and goings, see what he gets up to when he thinks no one is watching."

Great. Here we go again. Balor was going to order me to sneak around Fionn again, and if I screwed up? No telling how he would react. This was a terrible idea, but at least it meant action. Sitting on my hands would only drive me crazy.

"What time are we—" I started to ask, but Balor cut me off with a flick of his wrist.

"You won't be going," he said sharply. "Not after your performance. I'm sending Cormac and Lesley instead. The rest of you…get to work finding out anything you can. Watch the footage again. Go through their rooms. Duncan, come with me. You'll be on duty at the front door for the rest of the day."

~

Moira and Elise threw open my door and strode inside with a stack of pizzas towering between them. We'd spent the past ten hours combing through video footage, hoping to find something that Lesley had missed. No such luck, not from any of the three nights the fae had gone missing.

"We've come bearing gifts," Moira said, shrugging off her jacket and tossing it onto the coat rack in the corner.

Elise plopped the pizza boxes onto my side table and grinned. "We thought you could use some cheering up after you got chewed out by Balor. And after the training thing. He can be a hard-ass when he's really trying to make someone improve. But he's just doing it because he cares."

I raised an eyebrow. She was so very, very wrong. "Doesn't really feel like he cares at the moment."

Moira and Elise exchanged a glance. "I think your lack of training worries him, especially after the fight you got into at his club. He's just trying to make you stronger."

"Hmm." I flipped open the box and grabbed a slice of pizza. My stomach rumbled. All the training and the mission-planning had left me famished, as per usual. "I'll have to take your word for it. Right now, it feels like I'm a target for his irritation."

"Three of his fae are missing," Moira said with a sad smile. "He's going to be especially touchy for awhile, particularly if we don't find them soon."

I paused my chewing. "I really don't understand what happened. They couldn't have just vanished into thin air. How did someone manage to take them from their rooms inside a well-guarded House? And not just once. *Three times.*"

Elise's eyes dropped to the carpet. "I've got to be honest. I'm getting pretty worried. I try to put on a happy face in front of the others, but things aren't looking good. If we don't find a lead fast, then…What if they're dead?"

She trailed off, her voice cracking on the last word. My heart went out to her. If *I* was worried about Ondine, I couldn't imagine how she felt. She'd known all three of these missing fae. She'd lived with them for decades. They were part of her family, her life.

I reached out, took her hand, and squeezed. "Well, we just have to keep trying. We don't give up until we find them, okay?"

Moira nodded. "Damn straight."

Which meant one thing and one thing only. I was going to have to go to the catacombs tonight and see what Tiarnan was up to. I mean, I had planned on going anyway, but listening to Elise had only strengthened my resolve. Tiarnan might not be the abductor, but maybe he would lead me to the fae who was.

15

It was easy enough to sneak out of the House undetected, and hopefully, it would be fairly easy to slither back inside. Duncan was still on guard duty for the evening, but I waited to make my exit until he left the front door to do a sweep of the rear corridors. Balor would probably come looking for me first thing in the morning for more training, but I'd be back in plenty of time to be ready at six.

Hopefully.

It took twenty minutes on the tube for me to get from the renovated power station that was home to the Crimson Court and down to West Norwood. When I stepped out onto the sidewalk, I found myself on a quiet High Street with a few open pubs. The pavement was empty and only the occasional car whooshed by, tail lights bouncing on the dark road.

I shoved my hands into my jacket pockets and hurried toward the cemetery entrance a couple of blocks away. Halfway there, I spotted a familiar figure up ahead. His gaze was focused hard on the tall brick wall to our right, giving me the perfect view of his profile.

Sharp cheekbones, strong jaw, impossibly dark hair that blended into the night. It was Tiarnan.

My heart sped up along with my feet. I glanced at my watch. Midnight. He was right on time. For some reason, he had come to the cemetery catacombs in the middle of the night. Alone. I'd half-expected to see Fionn or another one of his warriors by his side, but no one was there. And he looked more than a little jumpy.

I frowned. Could he actually be the one behind the missing fae? It seemed so unlikely, and nothing I'd heard from his mind suggested he was capable of that kind of crime.

Suddenly, Tiarnan shifted toward the right and disappeared into the shadows. I swore underneath my breath and picked up my pace. I couldn't let him out of my sight. I needed to see what he was up to. The gates to the cemetery were just up ahead, but he hadn't reached them before he'd swerved off the path.

I slowed to a stop when I reached the spot where he disappeared. A hand lurched out from the darkness. I bit back a scream and jumped back, but it was too late. The hand wound tight around my arm.

Tiarnan yanked me forward. I stumbled into the bush where he'd been hiding, thorny branches scratching my pristine jacket. Balor wasn't going to be happy when he saw I'd already ruined a uniform. But that didn't matter. Not when I was being attacked by a Fianna warrior who probably wanted to toss me into his dungeon of doom.

"What are you doing here?" he asked with a frown. "Are you following me?"

"Who me? I'm just out for a nighttime stroll." I yanked my arm out of his grip, doing my best to mask the terrified beating of my heart. "Now, if you'll excuse me—"

"Don't." He went quiet when footsteps sounded on the pavement just beside the bush, and then vanished into the distance. "Let's not play games. You're following me. Why?"

This could only go a few ways. Either he was the abductor—and potentially a murderer, too—on his way to visit the dungeon where he was hiding his victims, or he was *helping* the abductor. I couldn't really think of another reason why he'd be here. To visit a buried relative? That seemed like an unlikely thing to do in the dead of night.

Still, might as well be honest. At this point, lying wouldn't do me any favours. "A little birdy told me that you were heading here tonight. I thought I'd see what you were up to."

"A little birdy." He crossed his arms over his thick chest. "Only one other fae knows I was coming here tonight, and I find it hard to believe that he would tell you my plans."

I shrugged. "I don't know what to tell you."

"Fine," he said. "It doesn't matter. I'm going into the catacombs. If you insist on coming along, I won't try to stop you."

I arched an eyebrow. Again, kind of a suspicious thing to do. Maybe he hoped he could lure me down there. Then, he could knock me out without the risk of a random human passerby seeing a damn thing.

Pursing my lips, I pressed into his mind. It was more difficult to read him now than it had been before, a sign that he wasn't entirely comfortable with my presence here.

Of course, I *had* dumped a crimson drink on his head at the bar, so…

How did she find out I would be here? I really shouldn't let her come with me, but I can already tell that nothing I say will stop her. Maybe it's for the best.

That…didn't really clarify a damn thing. *Come on, man. Give a girl a break. Make your thoughts clearer. Either think about the fact you're going to try to kill me or think that you're definitely* not *the culprit.* I needed something crystal clear. I was tired of having to translate these riddles.

That was the problem with reading minds. You didn't always hear relevant information.

But Tiarnan wasn't going to make things easy on me. He took off down the pavement, stopped at the gate, and hauled himself over the metal bars before I could get any more thoughts out of his brain. With a sigh, I followed after him, though I wasn't nearly as graceful with the whole scaling a metal gate thing. I scrambled over the top, legs and arms akimbo, and fell flat on my back on the other side.

For the second time in one day.

Ouch.

"Honestly," Tiarnan said, rolling his eyes and holding out a hand. "One might think you're not fae."

"I'm only half-fae," I said, brushing the dirt off my trousers. "I have a shifter side that keeps me from experiencing some of the more useful fae skills, like…I don't know, always landing on your feet."

"Now I see why you ended up in Balor's House.

He has a soft spot for shifters." Tiarnan grasped my hand and pulled me up from the ground. "Anyway, we don't always land on our feet. We just spend a lot of time training. You'll get there in time."

I wasn't so sure about that.

"Come on. The catacombs are this way." Tiarnan led me through the maze of pathways that wound through the heavy darkness of West Norwood cemetery. I'd heard about this place, but I'd never been here before myself. It was on the list of London's Magnificent Seven Cemeteries. Yes, that was a list that actually existed. Morbid, I know.

Tiarnan stopped suddenly and pointed at a brick wall that was hidden behind rows of dilapidated scaffolding. "There's a set of stairs by that wall that leads down into the old catacombs."

"Really." I arched an eyebrow and crossed my arms over my chest. "Before I go down there with you, mind telling me exactly what you're doing here?"

"I thought your little birdy told you everything."

"Just tell me what's going on," I said. "And don't act like this isn't weird because you know it is."

He clenched his jaw, glanced at the grimy brick wall behind him. "Fionn got a tip-off about this place. The tip said that we would find some evidence here. Evidence that would lead us to your missing fae."

Huh. Well...that was unexpected. But also, "If that's the case, then why didn't you call Balor? The missing fae are from his House, not yours."

"They're from his House, but they're still from our Court, too. We care that they're missing, whether or not you believe it yourself. Besides, it was an anonymous tip. It could easily be some kind of prank or scam. Fionn thought it prudent for me to check things out before we brought anything to you."

"Hmm."

Tiarnan crossed his arms over his chest. "You don't believe me."

"I mean, it's a little bit weird, right? You coming here by yourself to check out some anonymous tip. Without telling Balor about it."

"Maybe Balor is the one behind it," he said in a low voice. "I hate to speak against my Prince. It isn't particularly honourable. But it's a possibility I cannot ignore."

I blinked. There was nothing I could really say to that. Tiarnan had voiced my suspicions out loud, but I couldn't bring myself to do the same. For some reason, I'd almost convinced myself that I'd been wrong, that Balor wasn't an abducting murderer after all. But it was weird. If someone knew something important about the missing fae, why would they tell Fionn instead of Balor? Unless they knew they couldn't tell Balor at all. Because he was the one who had taken the missing girls.

Unease swirled through my gut.

Tiarnan eyed me carefully. Darkness clung to his strong jaw, and his body was not much more than a silhouette in the darkness. "I won't ask you to speak your opinion on the matter. That would only test your bond with him, and we've both seen what that can do. Still, I can tell by the look on your face that you have the same damn suspicions that I do. No one knows where Balor was when any of the girls were taken. From his own House. Without being seen. Of course, no one has even asked him for an alibi. He's that untouchable."

Pain suddenly lanced through my gut, and my stomach felt ripped in two. Doubling over, I took a step away from Tiarnan to stop myself from throwing a fistful of dirt into his face. My bond pulsed through me, whispering at me to get him back for what he'd said about my Master, my Prince. He had to pay. He couldn't speak of Balor this way. I had to show him what traitors got when they spoke out against my Master.

"Calm down," Tiarnan murmured softly. "I won't say another word about it. The last thing we want is for you to go on some kind of rampage while we're in those catacombs. There's no telling what's down there."

The catacombs. Right. We needed to go down into the catacombs. With a deep breath, I rolled back my shoulders and shrugged off that intense energy that tempted me to lose my goddamn mind. Over Balor Beimnech of all people. *Come on, Clark. What the hell has gotten into you?*

A few days ago, I had hated him. Intensely. Now, magic was forcing me to defend his honour in the most violent of ways.

I needed to get a grip.

Together, Tiarnan and I found the stairs. They were hidden amongst thick greenery that climbed up the old, abandoned building's wall. Down into the darkness they went, curving toward the left where an arched doorway hulked in the shadows.

"Ladies first," Tiarnan said, motioning me forward.

"Fine." Why hadn't I brought that damn sword? Sure, I didn't know how to use it, but no one else had to know that.

Palms sweating, I inched downward. The steps wobbled under my boots, and I hopped down the last three just to get it over with. Amusement flickered across Tiarnan's face. He followed just behind me, and I took that moment to take another looksie inside his mind.

She's in desperate need of some training, but she sure is cute.

I sucked in a sharp breath, pulling my mind away from his as fast as I could. Heat poured through my neck and my face. He was pretty cute, too, but in a different way than Balor. My Master thrummed with power and energy, and his presence sucked up an entire room. Tiarnan seemed more...I don't know, boyish, even with his sharp cheekbones and chiseled jaw.

His muscles were just as massive, of course. And I needed to remember he was part of the most infamous warrior band around.

Tiarnan joined me at the bottom of the stairs and poked his head through the archway. I followed suit, letting my eyes adjust to the darkness. A tall central gallery stretched out before us, and three aisles branched off from each side. Down those aisles, I knew what we would find. Coffins. Lots and lots of coffins.

A scrabbling noise echoed through the dank space.

"Hmm," Tiarnan said. "Maybe that's just a rat."

"I'm not so sure this is a good idea anymore," I said quickly. "I was all in until two seconds ago, but something is *definitely* in there. Something bigger than a rat."

Tiarnan smiled and glanced my way, shadows highlighting the strength of his jaw. "You scared?"

"No," I said, and then cursed at myself. "Yes. Fine. I'm scared. Okay? If you aren't, then there's something incredibly wrong with you."

"I've been a warrior on many battlefields," he said quietly. "Catacombs are nothing compared to that."

There was sadness in his voice, regret. For once, I decided not to pry into his mind. It was clear that there were ghosts in his past that haunted him, despite how many years had passed by.

"Come on," he said, gently wrapping his hand around my arm. "Let's go see what we can find amongst the dead."

16

Tiarnan and I crept inside the catacombs. Water dripped somewhere nearby, the sound echoing through the dark space. Must filled my nose, a dusty, dank scent that could only be present in an underground tomb full of the rotting dead.

All along the walls, there were rusted metal gates that led to stores upon stores of coffins. A metal platform sat in the very center of the main gallery. What was it for? Not a clue, and I didn't want to ask.

"Any idea what we're looking for?" I hissed, leaning closer to Tiarnan.

He shifted to look at me, the shadowy edge of his nose only an inch from mine. "We're looking for something…off."

I rolled my eyes. Great. That was definitely a lot of help. Everything about this damn place was off.

We inched further down the gallery and turned right into the first corridor. A pool of blood spread across the middle of the dingy floor. My heart shuddered, and I took a step back, grasping tight onto Tiarnan's arm.

"Is that the kind of off you mean?"

He pulled the sword from his scabbard and held it high before him. It glowed, despite the heavy darkness. "Get behind me."

"Don't be such a dude. I can take care of myself."

"If you had a sword, I'd agree." He tightened the grip on his silver hilt. "Now, get the hell behind me, Clark."

I did as he said, but curled my hands into fists all the same. Every few feet, I cast another glance over my shoulder. Now, if I were the bad guy, I would have used this whole thing as some kind of lure. And then I would have jumped the unsuspecting snoops from behind them.

We inched past a floor to ceiling collection of old, rotting coffins. Cobwebs and dirt clung to every surface, but someone had placed a bright white cross on the ground beside them. Whoever had done it was probably trying to be nice, but…man, it just made the whole thing creepier, particularly because the blood had spread to the base of the cross.

"Shit," Tiarnan said, stopping suddenly.

I slammed into his back since I'd been paying far more attention to the cross. In that single instant where our bodies were touching, I couldn't help but notice how warm he was.

I shook my head and stepped back. "What?"

"Bodies. Two of them." He let out a shuddering sigh. "I recognise them. It's Rosalind and Abby. The missing fae."

I spun around him, heart in my throat. There, on

the ground just inside the nearest metal gate lay two female fae. Their matching brown hair had been arranged around their heads like halos, and their eyes had been covered by two golden coins. Their palms were facing the ceiling. And they were dressed in tiny white gowns.

Vomit bubbled up in my throat.

"This is disgusting," I said, blinking back the tears and turning away from the scene. "Whoever did this is sick."

And I hated myself, a little bit, for being relieved that neither of these two fae were Ondine.

"It is sick. Whoever did this deserves the full punishment of Faerie," Tiarnan said in a tight voice as he lowered his sword to the ground. "I have something to tell you. Fionn didn't tell me to come here tonight. I overheard him mention the catacombs in a conversation with someone else, and it made me suspicious. So, I decided to check things out, just to make sure that nothing was amiss."

I turned toward him, eyes wide. "You're telling me that you think Fionn is behind this? You think he's the killer?"

He lifted his shoulders, breath shuddering from his lungs. "Honestly, I do not know, Clark. Both of our Masters seem suspect. Balor could be behind this, but Fionn could be, too."

I couldn't argue with that as much as I wanted to.

"What should we do?" I asked just as my burner phone buzzed in my pocket. Frowning, I pulled it out and read the screen. It was Balor.

Shit. I would have to answer it. If I didn't, he would no doubt go into a frenzy and probably storm up to my room. Then, he'd discover I wasn't there. The only way to keep him from finding out I was gone from the Court was to answer the damn call.

Heart flickering, I put the phone to my ear. "Yes?"

"Where are you?" he asked, voice panicked, tone hard. "Where the hell are you, Clark? You weren't in your room. I thought you were gone. I thought you'd been taken. Lesley is missing, too, and—"

"Wait a minute," I cut in. "Lesley is missing, too?"

Tiarnan lifted his eyebrows, clearly intrigued. I motioned for him to stay silent and spun away to face the far end of the catacomb corridor.

"Clark," Balor said, his voice dipping into that low growl that sent shivers along my spine. "Answer my damn questions. Tell me where you are."

I bit my tongue. Balor was definitely *not* going to be pleased when I told him what I'd been up to tonight, and who I'd been with. In fact, I could picture his face now. That red flashing eye of his. Plus, I wasn't entirely ready to spill the beans just yet. He could be the killer. If he was, we needed to handle the whole thing…delicately. Or someone else would end up dead.

Lesley was missing now, too. Her life could depend on everything I said during this phone call.

"I think it's best if I explained in person," I finally said.

"Clark…" he said. "Tell me now or I swear I will make your life a living hell."

Despite my every urge to stay silent, the bond snapped tight between us, and words began to pour out of my traitorous mouth. Damn faerie magic.

"Okay, so I may have gone to the catacombs on a

hunch," I said, closing my eyes tight. "I got a tip. By using my power. And...well, I did what you asked me to do. Investigate what happened to the missing fae."

"*You're in the catacombs?*" I pulled the phone away from my ear and winced.

So...Balor wasn't happy. The thing was, if he was the one behind the attacks, I wasn't going to tell him over the phone what we'd found. I needed to look into his face—and his mind—when I told him what had happened to Rosalind and Abby. Once before, when he'd been in an emotional state, he'd let down his guard just enough for me to hear a snippet from his mind.

I sucked in a breath. I needed to play this right. "Listen, we did find something important, and we're on our way back. I'll be at the Court within an hour and—"

Suddenly, the line cut off.

"Hello?" I poked at the buttons, but nothing happened. Shrugging, I slid the phone back into my pocket and turned toward Tiarnan.

He'd gone deathly pale.

Slowly, he pulled a finger to his lip and pointed just over my shoulder. Dread pooled in my gut. Something was wrong. Something was very, very wrong. Death and decay curled around me like strands of fire, hissing whispered warnings into my ear.

I curled my hands into fists and carefully turned to face whatever lurked behind me. Three tall, thin, dark figures lurched down the corridor, their bony feet kicking up dust and dirt. I shuddered and stepped back.

"Sluagh," I mouthed the word, but I didn't dare speak it out loud.

Sluagh were…well, they were fucking zombies. An undead army of whittled bones and rotting flesh. Unlike the stories humans liked to tell, they didn't much like venturing above ground. Fresh air would tear at their limbs, making them disintegrate that much faster. They liked underground tunnels. Crypts and tombs…and catacombs.

I also hadn't thought there were any left in London. Looked like I'd been wrong.

"Ahhh," was all I could manage.

"You need to get behind me now," Tiarnan said, his steel whistling as he lifted it into the air.

"There are three of them. You're a great warrior, I'm sure, but—"

Tiarnan shoved in front of me, practically knocking me into the metal gate. I would have shot him an "ow" and a glare, but…well, we were about to fight a horde of zombies, so I was all out of snark.

The trio whistled toward us, arms outstretched, mouths open wide to reveal the fanged teeth that could cut human organs to shreds. With dark hoods and sunken eyes, they were like wraiths in the night. Zombie wraiths. Who wanted to eat us.

Tiarnan moved in almost silence. His sword whirled toward the Sluagh in a smooth, graceful movement that showed off the fact he'd practiced it thousands of times by now. But the Sluagh had swords, too, and they weren't afraid of death. The nearest Sluagh met Tiarnan's sword with one of his own while another swung his—or hers (I couldn't really tell the difference)—at Tiarnan's head.

Tiarnan managed to sense the sword just in time and ducked low to avoid the blow. Meanwhile, I just stood there like a helpless idiot watching the whole damn thing unfold.

I should probably do something. But what?

I got my answer two seconds later. Tiarnan used the ducking opportunity as a chance to catch one of the Sluagh off-guard, just like Balor had been trying to teach me. He swung out his legs, knocking the Sluagh to the ground. The creature's hands opened wide, and his sword clattered across the stone.

Bingo.

With a complete lack of grace, I snatched the sword and pointed it in the general direction of the melee. My heart charged like a runaway horse, and my skin felt as though it wanted to jump right off my bones and get the hell out of there. But I stood my ground, taking short breaths in and out of my nose.

The Sluagh whose sword I'd stolen rose slowly from the ground, his tangled, matted hair hanging in front of its sunken face. It looked like something out of a horror movie. Hell, it looked far, far worse, because it was very much real and standing right in front of me, clearly pissed off that I'd stolen its sword.

I pointed the thing at its chest, and I swore a haggard laugh wheezed from his body. Shivers raced down my spine.

Out of the corner of my eye, I saw Tiarnan glance in my direction, and then he swore. "If you're going to wield it, at least hold it like a damn sword instead of a pencil."

I scowled in his general direction without removing my eyes from the creature. Okay, so he had a point. With a deep breath, I pulled the sword back and held it aloft like I'd seen him do earlier. My arms shook. The sword was a hell of a lot heavier than I'd expected.

The Sluagh was still sneering at me, but he wiped that look right off his face when I swung the sword his way. It careened wildly, and my fingers almost lost their grip. My opponent jumped out of the way, cackling wildly.

Dammit. I caught my balance and took two steps back. The Sluagh followed. He clearly didn't consider me a threat, even if I did have a death grip on his sword.

And he was right.

Unfortunately, Tiarnan was still engaged in his own fight against the other Sluagh. One he'd already managed to dispose of, and its broken body now lay on the stone floor. But the other was still going strong. Their swords clashed hard as they parried their way through the catacombs.

Perhaps it was time to try a different tactic. Tightening my grip on the hilt, I narrowed my eyes and turned my mind toward the creature before me. Darkness hissed along my skin, and a strange power rippled as I poked into the depths of the Sluagh. That power poked back with a sudden bite, vicious and angry and strong.

I blinked.

In all my years, I'd never had that happen. It was if the Sluagh had erected some kind of mental wall, one that went into fight defence mode when prodded. It was different than what happened when I tried to read Balor. He was just a blank wall. A nothingness. A hard rock that couldn't be moved.

This? Well, it freaking hurt my head.

I was still reeling from the mental bite when the Sluagh launched itself at me. It knocked me flat on my back. My breath whooshed from my lungs from the painful smack. The sword spun away from me, hurtling away from my outstretched hand.

"Clark!" Tiarnan shouted just as the Sluagh jumped on top of me. It hissed as it leaned down to stare into my face, saliva dripping from its sharp teeth.

I shivered and turned my face away so that my cheek smashed against the rough stone. The bodies of the dead fae were only a few meters away, and my stomach twisted in on itself from both the horror of their fate and my own.

Suddenly, the weight on my body disappeared. Sucking a breath into my lungs, I scrambled back to see that Tiarnan had slung the creature away from me. Now, he was fighting two of them, and I was weaponless. Again.

"Get in the coffin room," Tiarnan shouted as one of the Sluagh managed to slice deep into his leg. Blood poured from the wound, crimson and thick.

"What?" I gaped at him.

"Get in the damn room!"

Did he mean the coffin room with the two dead girls? Surely he didn't mean that. But the Sluagh knocked him back a step, forcing me to retreat. I hurried into the room, peering out at Tiarnan through the rusted bars. His wound was oozing blood, and he was barely able to put any weight on his leg now.

Gingerly, he jumped back, joining me in the room. I slammed the gate shut behind him.

Without a word, I grabbed the nearest coffin and pushed it up against the gate to keep the metal firmly in place. And then the next, and the next, until there was a stack of coffins blocking the Sluagh from getting in.

Through the gaps, the Sluagh hissed at us, shoving their fingers inside to grab at our skin and our clothes. They couldn't reach us, but there was also no way for us to get out.

We were trapped.

17

Tiarnan slumped against the wall and slid to the ground. His face had gone bleach white, and his rapid breathing was more than a tad concerning. Fae lived long-ass lives, but they could be killed by most weapons. Unlike vampires, you didn't need a special stake to kill a fae.

I dropped to his side and frowned down at the blood coating his trousers. "I would ask if you're okay, but your wound answers that question easily enough."

He pried open his eyes, his jaw clenched tight from the pain. "I don't suppose you're a healer, are you?"

I winced. "No, my power isn't quite as helpful as that."

"I know. You're a mind reader."

"I...how did you know?"

"The look on your face earlier, when you met me outside of the gates," he said through shuddering gasps. "I've seen that look before. From another mind reader I know. She gets like that when she's trying to listen. I saw that, and then I thought about how you were at the club that night. It all makes sense. You were there to get inside Fionn's mind. To see if he's the killer."

The killer. I glanced at the fae bodies and felt my body turn to ice. We weren't only trapped by the Sluagh, but we were also stuck inside some kind of drop zone for a serial killer. If he came back while we were in here, he'd kill us, too. And we wouldn't be able to stop him. Tiarnan could barely breathe, and I had no weapon to fight him off.

We needed to get out of here. *Fast.*

Unfortunately, the Sluagh were still desperately launching themselves at the gates trying to get to us. We really were trapped in here, for god knew how long.

"Tiarnan, I don't know what—" I turned back to the male fae and fell silent. His eyes were shut, and his body had stilled. Sucking in a sharp painful gasp, I leaned down to place my ear against his mouth. The tickle of a breath whispered across my skin. I sighed in relief. He might be in bad shape and totally unconscious, but he was alive.

For now, anyway.

"Clark!" came a roar from somewhere deep within the catacombs. My heart lurched as I shifted toward the sound. I knew that voice. My soul recognised it in an instant. Power raced along my arms, and a strange urge came over me. To stand and walk—no, run— toward that voice as fast as I could. My soul felt broken, torn from its Master. And he was here to bring me back home.

I sucked in a sharp breath and shook those thoughts and feelings out of my head. It was that damn bond again, tricking my emotions into believing that I felt even a smidgen of affection toward Balor. I felt nothing toward him. Nothing but suspicion and doubt and distrust.

But…he was here. Looking for me. He could save us from these Sluagh. My heart tripped despite myself.

"Balor, in here," I called out to him.

I went as close to the gate as I dared and stared down the corridor. He emerged from the darkness, his entire being rippling with pure, unbridled power. Just looking at him made me shudder. He was strong, and sure, and he was *here*.

He'd come to save me.

Unfortunately, that also meant that the Sluagh had now turned their attention his way.

"Watch out!" I cried out through the bars as the creatures rushed away from the room where Tiarnan and I had hidden ourselves, their swords raised high in the air. They aimed their sights on Balor, on my Prince.

They reached him within an instant. A whirlwind of activity followed, but the darkness hid it all from my view. An explosion burst all around them, consuming them in fiery orange flames. The light blinded my eyes, and the heat rippled toward my face. I shoved the coffins away from the gate and stormed back into the corridor, rushing toward Balor.

But I needn't have bothered. As I stepped out of the coffin room, I found Balor standing before the fallen Sluagh, his shoulders heaving as he breathed. His eyes were fully uncovered, the bright red blinding as he stared down at the charred remains of the dead. Slowly, he slid the patch over his burning eye, and then lifted his other to meet my gaze from across the room. He took two steps toward me, dropped his sword, and placed both hands on my shoulders. My core tightened from his touch, even as fear shook through my soul.

"What the hell do you think you're doing here, Clark?" he demanded, though his voice was far softer than I'd expected. "You could have been killed."

I wet my lips and stared into his eye. This wasn't the reaction of a killer. It wasn't how he would have responded if he'd caught me here in his murder den. Instead, he was raw with a kind of emotion that made my heart quake. He'd been worried about my life. He'd come here to save me. And he'd unleashed the darkest part of his power in order to do so.

The fire of his burning eye.

"I'm sorry," I said, my voice cracking. "I was following a lead. Tiarnan, from Fionn's House, came, too. He's in there, and he's badly wounded. And…I have to warn you about something. We found Rosalind and Abby down here. They didn't make it, Balor."

He opened his mouth in a silent scream, and the spark in his eye cracked, as if his soul had been ripped straight from his body. And the roar that followed cut my heart in two.

~

An hour later, we were back at Court with the bodies of Rosalind and Abby. After Balor took a moment to get a handle on his emotions, he went into Prince and Master mode. He had driven to the catacombs and had told Duncan to wait outside. The two of them carried the wounded Tiarnan to the car, and when we'd returned to safety, Balor had ordered the Fianna to be taken straight to the healing ward.

He pulled himself together while everything was falling apart. I, on the other hand, felt like total shit.

I stood in the Court lobby, hands hanging by my sides as I watched Balor and Duncan carry the dead fae through the front doors. For some reason, I felt like it was all my fault, even though it wasn't. I'd been the one who had found them. After hiding things from Balor and suspecting him of being the killer.

He clearly wasn't. No one was that good of an actor. His pain had been real and brutal and raw.

Moira appeared by my side. Her cheeks were stained with tears. "You okay?"

"No." I shook my head. "You?"

"Not really. They were my friends. My family." She lifted her chin. "But we'll catch the asshole who did this, even if it takes us centuries. And it damn well might. Now that we've found them, he'll probably be even more careful to avoid getting caught."

"I'm sorry," I said. "I should have told you what I was up to."

Her eyes met mine, glittering. "Yes, you should have. We're your family now, Clark. Slinking off into the night without telling anyone, not even Balor, is not what we do here. We trust each other. We depend on each other. We can't do that if we hide things."

My heart squeezed tight. Little did she know that my sneaking around was only a small secret in a life full of them. Despite everything that had happened, I still hadn't told anyone about my power. That was due to Balor's orders, but still. It felt like a betrayal, particularly after everything that had happened tonight.

"Don't look so forlorn." She threw an arm around my shoulder and pulled me toward her. "Another thing we have here besides trust? Forgiveness. So, while it sucks that you didn't mention your little trip to anyone, I'm not going to hold it against you. Just… don't do it again, okay? You could have gotten killed. And I can't stand the thought of losing anyone else. Alright?"

"That's what Balor said." I sucked in a sharp breath. "He was…almost delirious, Moira."

"Speak of the devil," she murmured quietly, and then pointed toward the bottom of the staircase.

I looked up. Balor was there. Just looking at him made my heart hurt. The depth of his pain was reflected on his face, and I had the sudden urge to do anything in the world to make that grief disappear.

"Clark," he said in a weary voice. "Come."

18

I followed my Master to his office. He shut the door quietly behind us, and then went straight to the oak bar in the corner where he poured himself a massive shot of gin. Instead of tipping it back into his own mouth, he handed it to me, and then poured a second.

He raised the glass, waiting for me to do the same. I lifted mine and then drank the bitter liquid in a single gulp.

"Good." He took the glass from my shaking hands, and then poured me a second gin. After I'd had the next shot, I was feeling a little less on edge than I had moments before. But also way more aware of Balor's intense pull. My body wanted to go to him, to find comfort in the planes of his muscular chest… "Now, sit."

I did.

He sighed, leaned against his desk, and crossed his arms. When he spoke, his voice was cold, hard, and distant. "Explain to me what happened tonight."

I could see we were back to the orders instead of the questions. When he'd been worried about my safety, he'd lost the aloof commanding tone, but I was safe now. So, gone was any semblance of the fae who would rip apart the world to save one of his own.

I kind of liked that fae, even if he scared me.

"Okay, but you have to promise you won't freak out."

"I will promise no such thing."

I let out a sigh. "Fine. Just…please try to imagine things from my perspective when I explain them. You're not going to like what I have to say, but keep an open mind."

He didn't reply to that, so I had no choice but to plow forward. "I kind of lied to you about not hearing anything at your club the other night. When you sent me to spy on Fionn."

His nostrils flared.

"I mean, I wasn't totally lying. Some of what I said was true. I wasn't able to get anything from Fionn before I was kicked out. I tried to, but it just didn't happen. The thing is…I *did* happen to hear a few sentences from Tiarnan. It wasn't easy. Most fae are kind of hard to read, including him. So, I only managed to get a few snippets."

"You actually heard something that night?" he asked in a low growl.

I winced, and then nodded. "Tiarnan was thinking about what he did and didn't want to tell me. One thing he wanted to keep hidden was the fact he planned on heading to the catacombs at midnight tonight. I thought it was kind of a weird thing to have planned, so I decided to see what he was up to. Just in case."

"Just in case he was the killer," Balor finished for me, his hands closing into tight fists. "And you didn't happen to think I would be interested in this information?"

"Well." I wet my lips. We were closing in on the part that was probably going to piss him off. "Truth was…I didn't know if I could trust you."

He stiffened, and his spine went stick straight. "You didn't know if you could trust me? I am your Master, Clark. Your Prince. Of all the fae in the world, I am the one you should trust over any other. I don't understand why you would—"

"I was worried you might be the abductor, okay? And to be honest, I was scared that whoever had taken the girls was killing them, too. As it turns out, I wasn't wrong to be worried about that. Just…well, I was clearly wrong to think it might have been you."

I gritted my teeth and hunkered down in my chair, bracing myself for his fiery reaction.

"Explain why you thought it might be me," he said, his voice as icy as the frozen winter ground.

"You're known to kind of have a thing for brunettes. Every single fae who went missing? Brunette. You're scarily powerful. Everyone knows that. And well…no one knows where you were when they were taken. They disappeared from your House. There's no evidence on the tapes. You're one of the only fae who could pull something like that off."

Balor merely stared at me, and I could have sworn I saw disappointment flicker in his crimson eye. "You actually believe that I might be capable of something like this. That I would abduct and kill my own Court members."

"I..." I squeezed my eyes shut. "No, Balor. I don't. I mean, at first I did. Remember how I got attacked outside of Parliament? And then you magically showed up after I'd been knocked out? The whole thing felt fishy to me, I'm not going to lie. But...well, let's just say I don't feel that way anymore."

"You don't feel that way anymore," he said, shaking his head with a bitter laugh. "You know nothing about me, Clark. Nothing. I would do anything for my fae and my House. *Anything* to protect them. I would sacrifice my very soul to keep each and every single fae in this House safe."

His words held so much conviction, so much intensity. I could practically feel the strength of his emotions shivering across my skin.

"You know I should punish you for this." He pushed away from his desk and paced over to the window. "Fae have been banished for less. What you have done, what you have believed, many would consider it treason."

I sucked in a sharp breath. "That's not fair. I've only been here for a few days, and I had these suspicions way before I even joined your Court. My friend went missing for fuck's sake."

He whirled on his feet, arched a brow. "Your friend?"

Shit. In the heat of the moment, I'd forgotten that Balor probably didn't know that Ondine had been my mole. And now, it was too late to backtrack.

"Ondine." I stood, partially because I couldn't

stand sitting and staring up at him anymore. "She's my friend."

"I see," Balor said quietly, menacingly. "That certainly does explain things, such as how you got all your information in the first place. Don't think I didn't listen to your podcast."

"Don't blame Ondine," I said quickly. "She was just trying to do the right thing. She was worried about her fellow Court members and—"

"I'll deal with Ondine when we find her. Right now, I need to deal with *you*." Balor let out a low growl and stalked toward me, coming so close that his body shoved me up against the oak wall. That power that thrummed along his skin sparked to life, reaching out to shiver against my throat. I swallowed hard and wet my lips, a thrill shooting down my spine. Even though he was probably going to throw me back out onto the streets, it was impossible to ignore the electric current that passed between us.

Balor leaned down, and a delicious smile curled across his lips. "What's wrong, Clark? No snarky retort this time?"

"If you want to banish me, then I doubt there's anything I can say to convince you otherwise," I murmured, eyes locked on his lips, only inches from mine.

"Oh, I'm not going to banish you." His smile widened. "You're far too valuable to this Court. I won't let you go that easily, especially not when I'm certain others would like to snatch you right up. My enemies would love to get their hands on you."

I shivered. I didn't know what was worse. The idea of Balor making some kind of example out of me in front of his entire Court or some other Prince or Princess forcing me into their ranks. Ones who would use me as revenge against the Master I'd been bonded to.

The devil you know...

Balor pressed up against me, his muscular chest brushing against my peaked breasts. His eyes widened, almost as if something had suddenly surprised him. His gaze dropped to my lips, and his finger curled against my spine. "There is something about you, Clark..."

Suddenly, he pulled away. My body arched toward him, instinctively, but he was halfway across the room before I could even catch my breath. He moved to his desk and shuffled through the papers, scowling down at them.

What the hell had just happened? And why had he launched himself across the room to get away from me?

"You're dismissed," he said crisply. "Go get cleaned up and changed into some clothes that don't reek of Sluagh. We have a meeting planned with the rest of the team in an hour."

I frowned. "Okay, but what about—"

"Do not question me," he said in a snap. "I will have a think about your appropriate punishment and inform you when it has been decided. Now, *go*."

~

After I took a quick shower and changed into a fresh set of black guard clothes, I wandered through the glistening Court hallways until I found a sign that said Healing Ward, and an arrow pointing to the left.

As soon as I pushed through the swinging door, the entire ambience changed. Gone were the gold accents and glistening chandeliers. In their place was nothing but pristine white. White floors, white walls, white ceilings. Tiny windows lined one wall, looking out on a courtyard in the center of the property. Soft music piped through invisible speakers, and the sweet scent of lilacs drifted through the quiet space.

This was where I'd first stayed, on the eve before my trial. It felt like that had happened months ago instead of days.

Quietly, I strode down the hallway, peeking into empty room after empty room. They all had identical standard beds with crisp sheets and comfortable armchairs. Finally, a few quiet voices drifted my way. I followed the sound until I found a room halfway into the ward. Two fae stood over Tiarnan, fussing with his blanket. One of them I recognised. Deirdre, the nurse who had looked after me.

Both nurses turned toward me when they heard my footsteps. They had kind smiles and gentle eyes. A relief, since they were in charge of Tiarnan's life.

"How's he doing?"

Deirdre fussed with his pillow, and then said, "He's weak, and he did lose a lot of blood, but we've managed to close the wound."

"We're both strong healers," the male said. "He was almost gone when you got him here, but he'll be fine in a few days. He just needs some rest now."

Relief whooshed through me. I'd only just met the guy, but I felt responsible for what had happened to him. If I hadn't been there, he probably would have been fine. It was only trying to save me that got him into this situation in the first place. I'd gotten in the way, and he'd paid the price.

"Unfortunately," Deirdre said, "he's still unconscious. You can sit here with him for a moment if you like, but he won't be responsive."

"I....no, that's okay," I said quickly, taking a step back out of the door. Tiarnan probably didn't even want me there. He needed someone he knew. Someone from his House. But his fellow fae were probably going to be super pissed off when they found out he was doing his own little spy recon mission as a way to investigate his boss. "Just wanted to make sure he was okay."

"When he wakes up, we'll tell him you stopped by, Clark," the male said before turning back to the patient. Because of course he would know my name and who I was. And he probably had a pretty good idea that I'd gone rogue tonight. Did he hate me? Did they *all* hate me?

And why did I even care? As soon as I found Ondine, I was out of there.

Nothing had changed, even though it felt like everything had.

19

"Tell me how long it has been since Ondine disappeared." Balor braced his hands on the table in the command room and glared in Kyle's general direction.

"Er, it's been about seventy-two hours now," Kyle said.

"Seventy-two hours," Balor said slowly, looking at each of us in turn. When his eye reached me, he lingered for a moment longer before moving on. "Ondine was not found in the catacombs with Rosalind and Abby, which suggests that she may still be alive. However, I fear we don't have long. And now, Lesley is missing, too. She fits the profile. The same fae has no doubt taken her as well."

Moira punched the table. No one chastised her for it, not even Balor. I was pretty sure we all felt the same urge to punch something, preferably the killer's face.

"I have a question." Elise raised her hand with a weak smile. "How exactly are we going to find Ondine and Lesley before he kills them? We don't even have any leads. I checked Lesley's room myself. There's nothing there. No sign of her on the security cameras. She and Cormac had just gotten back from watching Fionn, but they both said nothing interesting happened."

"We do have one lead," Balor said, glancing at me. "Clark. Explain what you discovered and how you discovered it."

I blinked at him. Was this some sort of trick question? Or worse, a test? He'd made it clear on more than one occasion that he didn't want me to tell a soul about my powers, so surely that's not what he meant. Of course, I couldn't read his freaking mind in order to get some clarification.

Slowly, he gave a nod. "Yes, I do mean what you think I mean. Tell them about the night at the club. Tell them what you heard and how."

"Er…"

Moira cocked her head. "What's he talking about, Clark?"

Great. So, this was it then. The moment they all decided they hated me. Knowing that they would pull away from me now upset me far more than I expected it would. Even though I would leave the Court once all of this was over, I didn't want these fae to hate me. Moira and Elise, especially.

"Right, okay, I guess this is happening." I sucked in a deep breath before adding, "Just so you know, Balor asked me not to tell you about this. Otherwise, I would have by now. Probably."

"Clark. There's no need for commentary," he said. "Tell them."

"So, this is where I tell you that my power is the

ability to read minds," I said in a rush of words. "Most minds. I can't read Balor's. Anyway, since you all suspected Fionn of being involved in the disappearances, Balor asked me to go to his club the other night to see if I could pick up any useful thoughts."

"Wait a minute." Elise placed her hands on the table, leaned forward, eyes sparkling. "You're saying you can read minds? Daaaaaamn. No wonder Balor put you on the investigation team."

I blinked at her. "You're not...I don't know, weirded out?"

"Eh, not really," she said with a shrug. "As long as you don't constantly go digging through my head, then I think it's sweet. And incredibly useful."

I glanced at Moira.

She also shrugged. "What you see is what you get when it comes to me. Go digging around in my head all you want. You won't find anything I wouldn't say out loud."

Kyle raised his hand and gave me a sheepish grin. "I'll admit it weirds me out a little, but I don't really like sharing. That said, it's not any scarier than Lesley's power."

"Which is?" I asked, eyebrow raised.

"She can stop people's hearts with a single touch. That's why she wears gloves all the time."

Right. Well, I'd have to make sure I stayed away from her hands then. Once we found her.

Duncan and Cormac were both silent, but they were usually silent anyway.

"They'll come around," Elise said with a wave of her hand. "Back to the story. You went to eavesdrop on Fionn's mind. What did you hear?"

"Well, that's part of the problem. I didn't hear anything from him. I didn't really have a chance to because I got kicked out, remember?" Now it was my turn to give everyone a sheepish grin. "But I *did* have a short conversation with Tiarnan, and I heard a little tidbit in his mind about how he planned to go to the catacombs."

"So, Clark decided to follow him." Balor took over, giving a little more information about what had happened in the catacombs. What he didn't do was put the blame on me, which surprised me. He didn't tell them that I'd gone without his blessing, and he made it seem as though I'd called him up for backup when I'd run straight into a den of Sluagh.

I decided not to clarify.

"There's obviously only one way forward," Duncan said when we'd finally finished explaining what had gone down in the catacombs. "If we don't move fast, Ondine and Lesley won't make it out of this alive. We need to make a move tonight. Fionn could have spotted Lesley and Cormac trailing him, so he decided to take her out."

"I agree," Balor said with a nod. "That is why we're all going to confront Fionn about this tonight, before he heads back to Ireland. You have thirty minutes to prepare yourselves. Make sure you're ready for a fight."

~

"Here," Moira said, tossing me a small black tank top. The two of us had moved into the sparring room to get ready while the guys were armouring up in the command station. "You need to put that on."

The fabric fell heavily into my hands. It weighed about five kilos more than it looked. "What's this about?"

"It's special armor. We save it for situations like this. No sword can penetrate it. You'll be a hell of a lot safer with it on."

Right. I kind of wished I'd known about this special armor before I'd launched myself into a den full of Sluagh. "How come you don't wear it all the time?"

"It works by drawing on our fae magic," she said. "If we wear it for long stretches, it can drain us to the point where we can't use our powers. In severe situations, we can even go unconscious."

"Right." I fingered the material, and then decided that Moira was right. This kind of situation called for some extra protection.

I pulled my shirt over my head and dropped it on the floor just as Balor strode into the sparring room. I froze, breath going still in my lungs. Blood rushed into my cheeks. All I could do was stand there like an idiot, half-naked in front of Balor Beimnech.

His eye flicked across my chest. I had on a black lacy bra, but it was a teensy bit see-through, and I knew he'd noticed. Probably because my headlights were blazing.

Moira cleared her throat. "Gotta go check on the others. Bye!"

And then she disappeared out the door. Traitor.

"Why," Balor began, stalking toward me, "are you half-naked in the sparring room?"

I wet my lips and lifted the new armour with a weak smile. "Moira said I should wear this instead of my usual shirt. I figured she was probably right. Since, you know, I don't know what the hell I'm doing when it comes to fighting. You said to be ready and—"

Balor snatched the shirt out of my hands and dropped it onto the floor. I swallowed hard, heart racing. He pushed up against me, took a free strand of red hair into his fingers, and tugged. Every single part of me melted onto the floor in an instant, my world disappearing into that blazing red of his eye.

"There is something about you, Clark."

He grasped the back of my neck and pulled my lips toward his. I tipped back my head, opening my mouth. His kiss was rough and hard, tearing into the very soul of me. My toes curled in my boots as I wrapped my fist around his shirt, clinging on tight.

If I let go, I knew I would fall.

Strength poured through me, filling me up from the inside out. His kiss deepened, his hand twisting tight around my hair. Every single part of me felt on fire, as if electric magic charged between us.

Once again, he pulled back and left me gasping for air. He stared at me, surprise and alarm flickering across his face. Rubbing his hand against his hair, he shuddered, as if the very act of separating himself from me was almost too much for him to bear.

Hell, I felt the same. My body yearned for him, so much so that I felt weak from being apart. Strength had flooded my veins, but now it was gone.

"What the hell was that?" I asked in a gasp.

He shook his head, took a step back. "I don't know, Clark."

I grabbed my shirt from the floor and shrugged it over my head. "You felt it, too, right? That…I don't know, that magic?"

His face suddenly clouded over. "I know what it was. It was a mistake. From now on, you should be more careful with your clothes."

He spun on his heels and stormed out, leaving me reeling. A second later, he was back. He strode straight over to the wall and grabbed a sword. It was the one he had pointed out to me earlier. It was long and deadly sharp with a silver hilt carved with elaborate swirls.

"You distracted me from the entire reason I came in here," he said in a cold, harsh voice that sounded nothing like the fae he'd been only moments before. "You need some protection. Even though you've had little training, you should take this with you just in case the worst happens."

I reached out for the sword, but he shook his head and held up a hand. "We may be rushing this, but we still need to do it properly. Kneel."

Right. So, two seconds after he kissed me and told me it was a mistake, he wanted me to *kneel* in front of him? Whatever, mate.

"This is tradition, Clark. Kneel."

I glared at him, and then huffed out a breath. Fine. Whatever.

So, I knelt.

Balor shifted closer. He placed his free hand on my right shoulder, and then on my left, murmuring underneath his breath. His words were far too low for me to hear, and while I tried to reach out for his mind, I found nothing but silence. As always.

"I endow you with this sword," he said, finally speaking loud enough for me to hear him. Gone was the coldness now. And the anger. Now, he sounded almost reverent. "You will be a weapon for this House, you will guard the fae who call this building home. A shield and a sword. The fire of the Crimson Court."

Shivers coursed along my skin, making every hair on my neck stand on end. Balor knelt before me and gave a nod toward my hands. As if I'd seen it done a hundred times before, I lifted both of my hands and held them palm up. I had no idea how I knew what to do, but I felt the motion of it deep within my very bones.

Balor placed the sword in my hands. Wind swirled around us, picking up my hair and blowing it across my face. My eyes met his, and for a moment, nothing else existed in the world but us.

"You are truly one of us now, Clark. Make it count."

20

Because of the weird independent relationship between Balor and Fionn, Fionn and his team of warriors had opted to stay elsewhere rather than inside of Balor's actual Court. There was plenty of room inside the renovated power station, but Fionn had insisted. It was a power move, according to Moira. A way for Fionn to remind Balor of their tenuous alliance. As long as Balor insisted on making nice with the shifters and the vamps, Fionn would continue to hold himself and his House apart.

So, that was where we were headed. To a boat that was docked on the River Thames, only a few blocks away. Fionn kept this boat in reserve for his trips to visit the Court. He and his warriors would be leaving by morning. Ondine and Lesley likely didn't have much time left, so it was go time.

We reached the boat after a ten-minute walk. I stared up at Fionn's strange home, awed by the way it glistened underneath the moonlight. It was a hell of a lot more elaborate than I'd imagined. It was a full-on million pound yacht with rose gold accenting the pristine white hull.

Fionn stood alone on the deck, hands in pockets, eyes trained in our direction. Wind rippled across his open shirt, showing off the muscles he must have spent hours perfecting. Another power move, no doubt. He wanted to show us that he was here, he was relaxed, and that he was powerful.

"How did he know we were coming?" Moira muttered underneath her breath.

"Clark?" Balor asked without turning my way.

With a deep breath, I focused on Fionn's mind, but there was a pavement, a body of water, and half a boat between us. "We're too far away for me to hear anything."

"Then, it's time for us to make our move," Balor said in a grave voice. "Remember the plan. Stay alert, be ready, and do not raise your weapons unless I give you the command. We need to give Clark time to extract the information we need to prove these fae are involved. Fionn's mind may be hard to read, and he likely won't bend very easily."

Fionn was waiting for us when we reached the top of the metal ramp that led from the shore to the deck. He still had his hands in his pockets, but his expression was anything but welcoming. His warriors fanned out behind him, each with swords slung by their sides. Their hands rested lightly on the hilts, but I knew they'd have their weapons out within milliseconds if we so much as breathed in the wrong direction.

So much for peace among the Court. Fionn was putting his toe far across the line. He wasn't fighting his Prince, but he was coming pretty damn close. One wrong move, and he'd be participating in treason.

Balor glared at the guards. "You will have your men stand down. I am your Prince, despite your independence, and you will show me and my House the respect it is owed."

"I don't owe you a damn thing, and you know it." Still, Fionn gave a nod toward his warriors. They stayed rooted to the spot, but they removed their hands from the hilts of their swords. "I was merely taking precautions. You brought *her*, even after what she did to us."

Fionn's piercing gaze moved to focus on me. I held my chin high, refusing to give him the upper hand.

"Clark is new. She did not intend to cause offence."

"Hmm. Where is Tiarnan, Balor?" Fionn said, suddenly shifting the conversation. "He is one of my most valuable warriors, and my most loyal. And yet he seems to have disappeared, like many of the females of your House. *After* he had a run-in with your new fae."

A commotion sounded from behind us. We all turned to find about a hundred humans clustered together on the pavement, staring up at us with wide eyes. Some held phones aloft, clearly recording this whole thing. The videos would be on Instagram and Twitter within seconds.

"Perhaps this discussion would be better suited for inside," Balor said slowly.

The humans were whispering now, pointing at our swords. We probably looked like some kind of team of avenging angels, which wasn't exactly a narrative we needed right now. Humans might tolerate us at the moment, but they probably wouldn't continue to do so if we went all sword-crazy in front of them.

Fionn clucked his tongue. "Fine."

He spun on his heels and motioned to his warriors. They nodded, leading the way down the wooden deck. The boat lightly bobbed in the water. It rocked just enough to make me feel the motion but not enough for nausea. That said, it left me a little bit out of my element. And I had to imagine it was the same for the others. Kind of smart, when I thought about it. Fionn's home turf was alien to us. If they trained on this boat, he and his warriors would have a big edge.

Just what we needed.

A serial killer with an edge.

When we reached the steps that led down into the depths of the boat, I hesitated. Duncan shot me a grim smile, and then nodded for me to move. The last time I'd gone "underground" things hadn't gone so well. And we could be walking straight into some kind of trap.

But down we went, regardless of the danger. I was beginning to realise that was just the life of a guard.

Below decks, Fionn motioned for us to sit among a cluster of cream leather sofas that stretched along the wall underneath a long thin row of windows. Through the glass, I could see nothing but pure inky darkness, the occasional bubble bursting in the deep blue.

Balor sat on the sofa, crossed one leg over the other, and leaned back while Fionn made them both a drink. He looked one hundred percent relaxed, the total opposite of everything I felt inside. My gut was churning. My palms were sweaty. Hell, my ears were even ringing a little.

I was glad I had a sword, even if I didn't know how to use it.

Fionn's warriors and Balor's guard team—including me—stayed standing. Both Masters seemed oblivious to the tension. Fionn swirled a drink, collected a second glass, and strode over to join Balor on the sofa. I decided it was now or never when it came to the whole mind reading thing. No one was really paying attention to me. All concentration was on the two Masters, as both teams tensely waited for a signal.

My breath shuddered from my lungs as I forced my mind to clear. As my body went rigid and still, I began to reach out toward the two Masters. I knew what I would look like now. Distant, vacant-eyed, and deathly still. Even though Balor had revealed the truth about my powers to his guard team, I knew it was still imperative to keep that detail hidden from this House. Especially if Fionn was behind the attacks. I couldn't let him know I was reading his mind. I remembered Balor's words. In and out, quick as lightning.

I had to work fast.

As I pushed my way toward Fionn, my mind slammed hard into a wall. Hmm. I pulled back and examined him closely. Fionn's mind was strong, just like Balor's. But where Balor felt immovable and as hard as a rock, Fionn felt more...like a cluster of pebbles that just needed to be kicked aside.

With a slight hitch in my breath, I pushed.

I cannot believe Balor brought that Courtless fae. A half-

breed at that. Filthy Carrion. She should be banished just for existing.

I sucked in a sharp breath and stepped back. My heart pulsed against my throat, and my ears roared. Everyone turned to look at me in unison, including the two Masters on the sofa. Balor met my eyes, his brow hiking up his forehead.

A silent question. Had I heard something that would implicate Fionn?

I shook my head, my heart still reeling from the impact of Fionn's words. What he had called me was the lowest of the lows. *Filthy Carrion.* Every supe knew what that meant, even me. It was the kind of term that you never, ever used. It was a curse. It was a death sentence. It was a term that sorcerers had used, a long, long time ago. It was a spell to condemn supes they felt didn't deserve to live. The deaths had been slow, gruesome, inhumane.

To use it against someone now? It was unheard of.

It made me feel as if I couldn't breathe.

Balor shifted back toward Fionn, frowning. "As I was saying, Tiarnan was under the impression that he would find something useful in the catacombs. I assume you were aware of this."

Fionn's eyes flickered. I reached out again, tempting the breach into his mind. It was still open, so I poked an ear inside, as much as I didn't want to hear his terrible thoughts.

How would Tiarnan have known about the catacombs?

Softly, I felt a flutter in my mind, as if Fionn had begun to turn toward me. I pulled back.

Out loud, he said, "No, I was not aware of this.

Hence, why I have been repeatedly asking you where my warrior is."

Fionn's tone was cold, harsh, and definitely disrespectful. Balor didn't do a damn thing to correct him, unlike what he did with me. There was a story here. A juicy one from what I could tell.

"Tiarnan is back at my Court in the healing ward," Balor said, watching Fionn's face very carefully. I could tell he was checking his reaction, hoping to see the truth hidden in the way his body tensed.

Fionn's cheeks went red, and his body began to tremble with barely controlled rage. "You took my wounded fae back to your Court and healed him without even telling me? Why? Are you trying to hide what really happened to him? Are you trying to protect *her*?"

Fionn pointed at me, his nostrils flaring.

Balor still lounged in his chair, his exterior the perfect picture of calm. "This is why we came. To tell you about Tiarnan. He will be fine. My healers are top class. It seems that Tiarnan was on to something when it came to the catacombs. He found two of our missing fae. Unfortunately, it was far too late to save them. They'd been killed and left to rot in the catacombs."

Balor paused, his attention slightly snapping in my direction. I took his cue and pressed back into Fionn's mind once again. This time, the metal wall was a little tougher. His mind pressed back against me, resisting my power.

I know you're in here, Filthy Carrion.

When I snapped open my eyes, I found Fionn staring right at me. He stood slowly from his seat, pointing an angry finger in my direction. "I knew it. I could feel it when you walked into the room. You're one of them. A mind reader. I should have known. And you." He whirled back toward Balor, his eyes flashing. "You brought her here so you could spy on my mind."

All pretence of calm and peace was forgotten as Balor stood. His voice bellowed when he finally spoke. "You act as though this is a surprise, Fionn. You have been actively working against me for years now. Then, I learn you know something about my murdered fae. I demand that you explain yourself. And be sure not to lie. Because Clark will know."

Ehhhhhh. I really wished he wouldn't put all the focus on me. Not to mention the fact that Fionn's mind wasn't exactly an open book. I couldn't just waltz on in like it was some kind of spring meadow full of blooming flowers. He was doing his darnedest to keep me out, and his mind was dark, dangerous, and full of daggers. Daggers that wanted me dead.

It was no use though. The damage was already done. Steel whistled through the air as the Fianna lifted their swords as one.

21

Balor stood his ground. All around me, the House Beimnech guards drew their swords. Power hummed through the boat, tension mounting with each passing beat. Trembling, I fumbled with the hilt of mine and followed suit. The sword was heavy, but I'd manage. At least I hoped I would.

Raising an eyebrow, Balor took a step closer to Fionn. The warriors shifted on their feet in response, but they did not swing their swords.

"Fionn," he said in a dangerous growl. "You dare have your warriors raise their swords at your Prince."

"My life is clearly in danger," Fionn answered in a snap. "They have been trained to protect me regardless of the consequences."

"They have been trained to protect Faerie, not you alone. And your life is not in danger unless you have done something that goes beyond treason against your own Court." Balor narrowed his eye. "If you killed those fae, it is treason against all of Faerie. And you know what that means."

A chill swept down my spine. Faerie was the combination of all of the Courts. At one point in time, there had been one central King, a fae who had stood as ruler for the entirety of us all. But that hadn't been the case for at least a century, if not longer. Now, the Courts were distinct, and Princes (and Princesses) answered to no one. Still, the *idea* of Faerie had endured. If one was considered a traitor, their power was stripped bare, and then they were fed to the Sluagh.

A pretty insane kind of punishment if you asked me.

If I'd been Fionn, I would have felt more than a little unnerved. I probably would have backed the hell off and told my warriors to sheath their swords. Instead, he started laughing.

"Me?" he asked, pointing at his own chest. "You think *I'm* the one who is a traitor to Faerie? Last time I checked, great Balor 'the smiter' was the one making friends with bloody shifters. If there's a traitor in this room, it damn well isn't me."

Balor growled, threw back his shoulders. Power pulsed against the walls, causing the boat to tip sideways. "*Enough.* For too long you've tried my patience, Fionn. I will no longer allow you to make a spectacle just because of who you are. Clark, come here."

I blinked at him. "Say what?"

It had kind of seemed like I might get out of this little rendezvous without getting punched, clawed at, or trapped in a metal cage with dead bodies. The attention was on someone else for once. Fionn. And I preferred to keep it that way.

"Come here," he said through gritted teeth. "Do not even contemplate trying my patience, too."

Wincing, I quickly stepped over to his side. My pulse raced, causing my skin to bounce against my veins. Balor was pretty pissed off, and Fionn was, too. Not to mention all the Fianna, and the House Beimnech guards. And, once again, I'd somehow become the center of attention.

Bloody brilliant.

"Read his mind," Balor said without a single glance in my direction. "Find out if he's the killer."

Errr. Now, wait a minute.

"Are you sure that's a good idea? He—"

"Read his damn mind, Clark," he said so loudly that I jumped in my skin.

"Don't you *dare*." Fionn lifted his chin as I turned toward him. "Stay out of my damn mind. You don't have to listen to him. He's filth. He's a traitor to Faerie."

My blood began to boil, the magic of the bond snapping tight at his words. Frowning, I lifted my own damn chin and glared at him. "Sorry. I don't listen to you. Balor's my Master. Besides, I heard what you called me. Karma's a bitch."

Pulling air into my lungs, I closed my eyes. Now that I stood only meters from Fionn, it only took seconds for me to reach the uneasy wall he kept erected around his mind. Emotions were charging through him, which made his barriers a little weaker, a little less certain. He was angry, and he felt betrayed. I could read all that without hearing a single one of his thoughts.

I pushed a little against the wall, expecting him to fight back. But instead, he just let me in.

Hello, Clark. I assume you want me to conveniently think about the killings so that you can determine whether or not I'm behind them. You, as a mind reader, should know it isn't that easy to pluck the truth from someone's thoughts.

Inwardly, I frowned. This was certainly a first. I'd never had an actual *conversation* with someone in his own mind, and I didn't quite know how to handle it or what it meant. Could someone lie in their head? Probably. Maybe? There was no way to know. And honestly? I was kind of creeped out.

If you aren't behind the murders, then you won't care if I read your mind.

A flicker of irritation followed. *You may have a point. That said, I'm certain you know how people feel about mind readers. You cannot honestly tell me that everyone you've encountered in your life has been happy about you digging around inside of them.*

It took all my self-control not to pull out of Fionn's head. He was far too close to the truth for my comfort. Of course people had hated it. And I'd pushed more than one friend away because of what I could hear. The wounds were still fresh, the trust so raw and broken.

The sooner you give me access to the truth, the sooner I'll be out of your mind. I think you know as well as I do that Balor won't stop until he gets what he wants.

Another flicker of irritation, but a moment later, another wall fell away. This time, what he showed me was more than just a thought. A memory, visually, sprang up in my own mind. The setting felt familiar.

Fionn was striding down the pavement in London, speaking to one of his warriors.

"Apparently, Balor has found himself a Courtless fae, as unlikely as that is," Fionn said with a sneer. "With any luck, we'll get her, though he's probably rigged the trial to his advantage."

I frowned at that, but kept watching.

Fionn's phone rang. He held it up to his ear. "Fionn."

A tinny voice answered, one disguised by some kind of machine. "If you want to know what has happened to the missing fae, you need to investigate the West Norwood catacombs." A pause. "Do not tell the Prince."

The memory snapped away, and I pulled myself out of Fionn's head. The two of us stood staring at each other. His jaw was clenched tight; his eyes were hard. But I knew there was fear hidden behind the bravado. He thought I might screw him over, tell Balor that he was behind the murders, even though he wasn't.

Fortunately for him, I was a better fae than he was.

"Well?" Balor said, snapping me out of the moment. "Tell me what you heard."

What *had* I heard? Fionn's mind was strong, and he'd been able to speak to me through my power. If he could do that, could he trick me with a false memory? It wouldn't be that difficult to do, if you'd been trained and you knew exactly how to fake it.

I was going to have to trust my gut on this one.

"He's not the killer," I finally said. "Fionn got an anonymous phone call that tipped him off about the catacombs. The voice he heard was weird, like it was being disguised by one of those machines in scary movies."

"An anonymous phone call," Balor repeated before closing his eyes and letting out a heavy sigh. He almost seemed...disappointed.

"If it's not me, then who is it?" Fionn spoke out loud this time. "That's what you're thinking, isn't it? Truth be told, I thought it was you, Balor. Hell, maybe I still do. This could all be some kind of charade to trick your Court into thinking you're safe."

Duncan suddenly growled from behind me and stalked toward Fionn with his sword raised. "You dare question our Prince again, after he has given you the command to stand down? After he has given you more than ample chances?"

The Fianna surrounded Duncan within a moment, swords all pointing right at his throat. All around me, the House Beimnech guards whirled into action. They aimed their swords at the Fianna. My heart hammered as I took in the scene. Things were clearly escalating, and not in a good way. Everyone was pointing their swords at everyone else, and all it would take was one wrong breath, and the whole thing would descend into vicious fighting.

"Um, hi." I held up my hands from the center of the sword fest. "Look, I know everyone is on edge right now, but don't you lot think it would be better if we just lowered the weapons? No one really wants to hurt anyone here, right? We got our answers about what Fionn knows. And Fionn now knows where Tiarnan is. Why don't we just...back off?"

No one said a word. They all just looked at each other, tension bouncing through the boat.

Finally, Balor spoke. "Do as Clark says."

After a long, excruciating moment, Elise was the first to lower her sword. Kyle followed, and then Moira after that. Finally, everyone stood with their weapons pointed at the ground instead of each other.

That said, everyone was still pissed as hell.

"Don't think this changes anything I've said, Fionn," Balor said. "You and your warriors are on thin ice now. I cannot trust you. Not after the way you've behaved tonight."

"Great," Fionn replied with an icy smile. "That makes two of us. My House will learn of everything that has happened here tonight. Especially how you carry your new mind-reading toy around with you." His grin stretched wide. "I wonder, when will you take her to bed? Does she know that once you're done with her, she'll be nothing more than rubbish? She'll go straight in the bin, regardless of how useful she is."

With that, Balor lifted the patch from his eye and burned a hole in the side of Fionn's boat.

22

After Balor burned a hole in Fionn's boat, it was time to get the hell out of there. We left the Fianna to deal with the consequences, and then headed straight back to Court. Once I was inside the old renovated power station, I stormed straight to my room before any of my fellow guard members could get a word in edgewise. I was exhausted, mentally beat down, and more than a little confused about how I fit into this strange new world I'd found myself in. I didn't like what Balor had forced me to do, but worse, I didn't like that I'd *wanted* to do it for him.

And still, we were no closer to finding Ondine or Lesley. All we had now was a mysterious phone call. A voice that no one would ever be able to recognise. We were just as far away from learning the truth as we had been days ago.

I needed to rest my mind and my soul. I didn't know how I was going to sleep, but I had to try.

Unfortunately, fate had other plans for me. Or at least Balor did. He whispered into my room without knocking. Thankfully (maybe), I hadn't yet torn off the tank top armor.

"Balor," I said with a heavy sigh, crossing my arms over my chest. "Why are you here? I just want to mope in peace for awhile, okay?"

"You seem upset," he said quietly. "Did Fionn's words bother you?"

"Well done, Sherlock. You'll make a PI just yet."

He pressed his lips together, his eye following me as I tossed the sword into the corner of my room. Technically, I was supposed to return it to its place in the sparring room unless I was out and about on a mission, but I felt a hell of a lot more secure with it by my side.

And I needed some security after the past few days.

"I'll choose not to take your anger personally." He leaned against the wall, crossed his ankles. "I saw the look on your face when you entered Fionn's mind. You heard something else that you didn't want to mention while we were there. Something that upset you."

I busied myself with the leftover pizza box. Damn I was hungry. Me, the Filthy Carrion. "I don't want to talk about it."

"Clark." Gently, Balor took my hands in his and forced me to face him. It was hard to look at him. Not just because of our charged moment in the sparring room but because of what he'd ordered me to do, of what Fionn had said about him discarding me like a piece of rubbish. I just felt so on edge around him, like his very presence picked apart the fabric of my soul. That single eye of his saw so much more of me than anyone else ever had, and I couldn't say that I liked it.

In fact, it terrified me.

"Tell me what you heard," he said quietly. "It could be important."

"Right. *Important*." I let out a harsh laugh. "For a second there, I thought you wanted to know because you were worried about my feelings. But no. You only want to know what I heard because you think it affects you and your Court."

"You *are* my Court, Clark." He gripped my shoulders tight in his hands, and his forehead dropped to mine. "Why can't you understand that? Why can't you believe that I care? If you overheard something that upset you, I need to know about it. It's important because of you."

I blinked up at him and wet my lips, my cheeks stained with pink. "He called me a Filthy Carrion. You know, the old sorcerer curse. It just took me by surprise, that's all. I've never actually heard someone use that term, not even in their minds. And I've heard people call me a lot of things. Trust me. By now, I've pretty much heard it all."

"I'm sure you have," he said quietly, his jaw clenching. "I'm sorry you had to hear that. Fionn was out of order tonight. He has been for a very long time. I will make sure that he answers for what he called you."

"No," I said quickly, reaching up to wrap my hand around his. "I don't want you to do that. I don't want him punished. I'm used to it, okay? I've never known anyone, not even my closest friends, to not think horrible thoughts about me. Only my—never mind. No one."

I'd almost mentioned my grandmother to Balor. A

bad idea, even though he wouldn't be able to figure out the truth just from that. My grandmother had always loved me, unconditionally. She'd never thought horribly of me, even when I'd been a brat. And I'd tried to find the worst in her, I had. I'd picked through her thoughts, seeking out anything that would prove she didn't care. And yet, I'd never found a damn thing. She had been patient, kind, and loving.

But she was gone.

"You're certain you don't want him to answer for that?" Balor asked. "It is an unforgivable thing to say."

"And yet, he *didn't* say it. Not out loud." I shrugged. "And anyway, things are strained enough now, aren't they? You burned a hole in his boat."

He let out a heavy sigh and dropped his hands from my shoulders, leaning back against the wall. "Relations between our Houses are far worse than they have been in a very long while. You did well tonight. Not only did you get the information we needed, but you prevented a fight from breaking out. If our Houses had come to physical blows, I fear that our Court would have been broken in two. The hole in the boat…well, it will cause issues, but it will not be the thing that tears us down."

"Yeah. About that." I curled my hands into fists, determined to speak my mind. "I don't like what you asked me to do."

He frowned. "I don't understand, Clark."

"You ordered me to force my way into his mind in front of everyone," I said. "It felt wrong."

He furrowed his eyebrows. "I don't understand how that's any different from what I've asked you to do in the past."

"He was standing right in front of me, like he was on some kind of trial." I shook my head, finding it difficult to put words to my thoughts. "I don't like to be so…aggressive with my power."

"I see," Balor said quietly. "And yet you would happily snatch at my thoughts during the single instant that I let down my guard."

"That's different."

He arched a brow. "How so? Is it fine as long as it's *my* mind you're waging war against, instead of someone else's?"

"Of course that's not it." But was it? I hadn't had any problem poking at Balor's brain, but the second he ordered me to do it toward someone else, I felt uncomfortable about it.

"Then, what is it, Clark?" He pushed off the wall and closed the distance between us. "I'm the only one you can suspect to be a murderer? Me, your Prince, instead of the male fae who would call you…well, I won't even speak that monstrosity aloud."

I fisted my hands, my entire body trembling. "I just don't like feeling like someone's pawn, okay? I've lived on my own for ten years. I make my own way. I do my own thing. If I'm going to poke around inside someone's mind, I want it to be on my terms."

"What happened to you?" he whispered.

Balor leaned down and cupped my face, his eye flicking between both of mine. "You're so closed off. You're so untrusting."

I arched an eyebrow, trying not to tremble beneath his touch. "Wouldn't you be untrusting if you could hear everything that people truly think about you?"

"Perhaps," he said in a low growl. "Or perhaps

there's something more than what you want me to see."

I shivered, but despite the fear pounding through my chest, I couldn't bring myself to pull back. Instead, I pressed up against him, breathing in his woody scent. He was jasmine blossoms and oak moss, vanilla and patchouli. Both sweet and heady at the same time.

I could get lost in his scent alone.

He shuddered as I placed my palms flat against his rippling chest. Maybe if I distracted him, he would forget this conversation, lose sight of the fact that I was hiding something big. Yes, that was why I wanted to curl up against his chest and feel his lips hot on mine. To distract him. Not because I actually wanted him. The one fae in the world I should—and could —never have.

"Clark," he murmured, rubbing a finger roughly against my bottom lip. "I am your Master and your Prince. This is dangerous."

"Maybe I like dangerous," I whispered.

Hell, maybe I really did. That was the only logical explanation for why I was throwing myself at Balor "the smiter" Beimnech, the Prince who had just forced me to go creeping inside of a rival's mind. The Prince who would decide I was no better than rubbish once he'd had me in his bed.

Balor leaned down and kissed me hard. I lost my breath, his heady scent filling my head. My blood roared through my veins, the peppery magic filling me with an impossible heat. The world around us whooshed away. Silence enveloped me. No thoughts, no words, no voices pounding against my mind's ears. It was just Balor. His lips, his tongue, his hands.

His body enveloped mine, and he slammed me hard against the wall. The wooden shelves beside us shuddered from the impact. Something fell on the ground, shattering through the moment. I reached out and twisted my hands around his neck. But it was too late.

Balor had already pulled back.

His eyes were wild; his cheeks pink. He no longer looked like the calm and in control Master of his House. He looked…ruffled. And I'd caused that. A bit of pride bloomed in my gut.

He ruffled his hair, his red eye sparking as he grasped my cheek once again. "I want this, Clark. I do. But you must swear you won't tell anyone about this. About us. The Court cannot know. It would cause issues."

I felt a little taken aback by that, even though I, of course, was only kissing him because of the whole distraction plan. Not because I wanted him. With a frown, I pulled his hand from my cheek. "Are you embarrassed of me or something? You don't want them to know you're into a Courtless half-fae?"

He gave me a look. "Of course not. But the Court expects certain things from me, and dallying with my own members is not part of that."

"Dallying," I repeated, eyebrow arched. I was really trying not to take this personally, but he was making that kind of hard. "Dallying, like you do with all those girls who show up drunk to your club on Saturday nights."

"Clark," he said, his voice a warning.

"Well, that's what you mean, isn't it?" I propped my fisted hands on my hips. "You're happy to be seen with them. Just not with me. I'm just 'rubbish' like Fionn said."

"You are jumping to conclusions."

"You know that was one of the reasons I was suspicious of you?" I continued, barreling forward even though I knew I should just keep my damn mouth shut for once. "You parade all these girls around at your club, but they don't seem to ever make it back to Court. Do you take them to some seedy motel? Or does a dirty alley do you just fine?"

Balor stepped back and straightened his shirt. His expression had morphed from pure fire to bitter ice. "I think that will be enough for this evening."

"Of course, there is another theory," I continued. "All that parading around is just for show. You never bring them back here, which means your reputation? It isn't the truth. You're not who you're painted out to be. But for some reason, you keep the lie alive. Why?"

Balor arched an eyebrow. "Any other theories?"

"No," I said, heart thumping.

"Good. Like I said, we're done here for the night. I'll let you keep your sword in your room just this once. After tonight, put it in the sparring room when it isn't in use. Goodnight, Clark."

And then he slammed the door, leaving me to stew in my own goddamn words. What had I just done?

23

"Hi." "Hi." Tiarnan shot me a smile. He was wide awake and propped up on a mound of crisp pillows, flipping through a magazine called Faerie Times while occasionally glancing at a nearby cell phone.

I edged into the room, not entirely sure if I was welcome or not. I had, after all, been the reason he'd ended up in the healing ward. "You must be feeling better now."

"Loads better, though I'm still a bit wobbly on my feet. The nurses say that I'll be good to go in the morning."

"Good to go. Back to your House, I'm guessing?"

His face clouded over, and he glanced at his phone again. "If Fionn will have me. He's not exactly returning my calls at the moment. Balor came by earlier and warned me about what happened. Apparently, Fionn is not pleased I went to the catacombs, not that I can blame him. I went behind my Master's back, investigated him, suspected him." He shook his head. "It was not honourable. I could very well be banished."

"I'm sorry," I said.

"Why?" He looked up and frowned.

I shrugged and edged further into the room. "For getting you into this mess. If it weren't for me, you wouldn't be in this healing ward. You stuck out your neck to save my life. I really need to amp up my training, that's for sure."

"You're forgetting that you aren't the reason I went to the catacombs in the first place. You're not why I was there. In fact, I think *I* should be the one apologising to *you*. I led you there. You could have gotten yourself killed."

"Well." I crossed my arms over my chest, a smile tickling my lips. "You're just going to have to deal with the fact that I'm apologising, okay? Accept it or I'll just keep doing it."

He let out a light laugh, his eyes sparkling. "You're pretty bossy for a girl who was a Courtless fae less than a week ago."

"Yeah, well." I glanced away. "I've never been particularly good at taking orders. The whole Master thing is pretty foreign to me. I guess I'm having a difficult time getting used to it."

"Luckily, I'm not your Master," he said with a grin. "So, you don't have to bow before me."

"Hey, you're not wrong." I grinned back. "On the other hand, you *are* a member of a rival House that I'm pretty sure just became even more of a rival. Maybe even an enemy. There was a whole thing. Swords were raised, holes were burned in boats."

"Soon to be an ex-member," Tiarnan pointed out before pushing himself up higher on the bed.

He peered up at me through long, dark lashes that highlighted the dark color of his eyes. I couldn't help but notice that Tiarnan seemed like the total opposite of Balor. Where the Prince was gruff and cold and unyielding, Tiarnan was open and actually kind of nice. He'd been a little on edge with me in the catacombs, but he hadn't known if he could trust me then.

Tiarnan cleared his throat. "Listen, ah, maybe I'm way out of line here, but I have a proposal for you."

I arched a brow. "A proposal?"

"Scratch that. Wrong word. Let's call it a question instead." He grinned. "If, in some hypothetical future world, I'm not banished from my House, and our Masters don't start waging war against each other, I'd like to see you again."

"I..." My cheeks went hot. *Oh.* What the hell was I supposed to say to that? And did I even want to see him again? He was the opposite of Balor, I had to remind myself, which meant he was probably everything I needed from a potential boyfriend. But wait. He'd just said he wanted to *see* me again. He hadn't mentioned anything about romance. Maybe he wasn't thinking of it as a date at all.

"Look, I understand your hesitation. We met under some wild conditions, and we barely know each other. Plus, we're from different Houses. But it's just one date, Clark."

A date. With a nice fae warrior who wasn't trying to find out my secrets, who wasn't pushing me away every chance he got, and who wasn't hiding darkness underneath his flickering red eye. A red eye that made my toes curl.

I looked at Tiarnan. He was handsome. There was no denying that. He had dark hair that curled across his forehead, and a smile that dimpled his cheeks. And he was honourable, at least from what I'd seen of him.

So, why was I hesitating?

Oh, right. I wouldn't be here very long. A little factoid I kept forgetting, but it was a pretty important one. I shouldn't start dating a guy when I planned to get the hell out of here as soon as I possibly could.

My hesitation had *nothing* to do with Balor.

In fact, screw the hesitation. Just because I planned to leave didn't mean I couldn't say yes. I mean, hell. It was just one date.

"Okay," I finally said, a smile slowly turning up the corners of my lips. "I'll go on a date with you. But you have to promise me one thing."

"Oh yeah?" He arched his brow. "And what's that?"

"As fun as that whole Sluagh thing was, I'd prefer if we go somewhere that doesn't involve the walking dead. No dungeons."

"You got it. No Sluagh. No dungeons."

So, I had a date. With a fae who wasn't Balor Beimnech. That was fine. It was more than fine. Balor had made it abundantly clear that he didn't want to date me himself, so why shouldn't I start seeing someone who actually seemed interested in me? There was no reason.

No reason at all.

At six-thirty the next morning, I strode into the sparring room to train with…well, myself. Balor hadn't shown up, not that I'd expected him to after what had happened between us the night before. I'd pretty much ruined any chance of a proper relationship between us, including one as trainer/trainee.

Not that it mattered. I was out of here soon, probably even before I had a chance to go on my date with Tiarnan.

No matter what it took, we *would* find Ondine and Lesley. Then, this Court and that insufferable Prince would only be a fading image in my rearview mirror.

In the meantime, I was going to learn how to use this damn sword. I had full access to the fae side of my powers now that I was part of a Court, and I needed to take full advantage while I still had them.

Unfortunately, I didn't know where to start. I sort of waved the thing around, trying to replicate what I'd seen people do in films. Jab, jab, slice. My arm ached though, and it was effort enough just to keep the damn thing from clanging against the ground. Jab, jab, owwww.

"Need help with that?" Moira asked as she strode into the sparring room, flipping her sword neatly from one hand to the other. I was crouched in an awkward squat, the sword raised in a weird half-hearted strike up at the ceiling.

I was pretty sure I was doing it wrong.

Also, I looked ridiculous.

The sword wobbled as I tried to hold it steady.

Moira chuckled, strode over, and took the sword from my shaking hands. Her golden hair was up in a tight bun, and she'd already donned some armor for the day. After what she'd told me yesterday, I was pretty sure that meant she expected a fight.

Moira wrapped both of her hands around the hilt. "First up. This is a two-handed sword. No sense in waving it around like some kind of dagger. You'll just hurt yourself if you keep that up, and you definitely won't be taking out any of your opponents."

"Right. Two hands. Got it." I rose from my crouch and brushed off my trousers. "Any more useful tips? I've been in here trying to teach myself, but as you can see, it's not going very well."

"Where's Balor?" Moira asked, glancing around the empty room. "I thought he was training you."

Er, how did I answer that?

I insulted him in every way possible. He was embarrassed to be seen with me. The two of us were like charging elephants that would just end up smashing the other aside.

"Balor and I have a complicated relationship," I merely said. "We may have had a little bit of an argument last night."

"A bit of an argument, eh?" Moira's eyebrows shot up her forehead. "About what?"

"Er. A lot of things." I cleared my throat. "Mainly about his reputation. As a man slut."

Moira snorted, blinked at me, and then tipped back her head. Her laughter echoed across the stone walls, her chest heaving as she gasped for breath. After a moment, she finally caught control of herself and gave me a look. "You actually called Balor Beimnech a man slut?"

"Well, not in so many words. But kind of?" I winced.

"I guess I got a little irritated with him. I don't understand what his deal is, and it's driving me crazy. I mean, does he sleep with tons of human girls? Or does he pretend to for some crazy reason? And if so, then why—"

I cut myself off there, but not quickly enough to avoid Moira's bright eyes. She opened her mouth, and then wagged a finger at me. "There's something going on between you two. I *knew* it."

My cheeks flamed. "Shh. Stop shouting. People will hear you."

"I see what's going on now," she said with an eager nod. "You two have a thing, but he doesn't want anyone to know. So, you got all worked up about it. Because of his apparent conquests and what Fionn said last night. The rubbish comment got to you, didn't it?"

"Are you sure you don't have mind reading powers?"

She snorted again. "I don't have to read minds to see how he looks at you. And you at him. Plus, he burned a freaking hole in Fionn's boat for talking shite about you. He wouldn't have done that for me or Elise. Trust me."

"Stop it," I whispered, though secretly, I kind of liked it. How exactly did he look at me? Inquiring minds...

"Listen, hot stuff," Moira said as she grabbed another sword from the wall. "Balor is a complicated lad. What you see isn't what you always get when it comes to him, unlike me. So, while I can't say for certain what his deal is with all the birds he pulls on his nights out, I do know that you can't always pay attention to public perception, if you know what I mean."

I scrunched up my face.

"In the fae world, PR does matter, Clark," Moira said. "Controlling the narrative. Anyway, you look like you need to punch something, so let's get to it before our morning meeting starts. Time to train."

And with that, Moira began to show me how to wield a fae sword.

~

We all stood clustered around Kyle's computer station. He tapped on some keys, glancing nervously over his shoulder every half second. Balor stood just behind him, arms crossed over his chest.

He hadn't looked at me since he'd entered the room. As always, he was impeccably dressed. He wore black trousers and a button-up black shirt that strained against the width of his biceps. Just last night, I had touched those arms and felt those lips against my skin.

I'd meant everything I'd said to him. I had questions. Ones he wouldn't answer, and ones I couldn't use to break into his mind. Did he really cycle through girls? If so, why would I ever let myself give in to him, particularly when he wanted to hide me from everyone he cared about? But, on the other hand, if he *didn't* do what he pretended to do, then why play the game? What was the point?

He was hiding something from me, and I was hiding something from him.

And I needed to remember the whole point of it.

If he found out who I was and where I'd come from, he wouldn't want to kiss me. He wouldn't want to take me to his bed. Hell, he wouldn't even want me in his Court. Gone would be the protector, the smiter of anyone who so much as looked at me the wrong way.

I would become the object of his wrath.

The very thought of it made my heart feel as though it was being split in half. The bond between us had strengthened in the past few days. It was hard to imagine it being gone. It hurt to think he could so easily cast me aside. I'd be banished. Or worse.

A traitor to Faerie. Stripped of power and fed to the Sluagh.

Balor must have felt my attention. He finally flicked his gaze my way. There was no softness in his expression. Not anymore. Frowning, I tore my eyes away from his face. I needed to get a grip. It wasn't as though I'd ever planned to stay here for very long. Why care if Balor wanted to keep his ex-attraction to me a secret? It was ridiculous.

I was ridiculous.

It was time to get a grip.

"Right." Kyle tapped the keys, a smile spreading across his face. "I'm getting close."

"Explain how this works exactly." I leaned down to stare at his screen. He had some complicated program running in the background, numbers whizzing by.

"When supes first came out to the public, Balor was smart enough to make a deal with Scotland Yard. The humans shared some of their technology with us in exchange for some information about a local vampire gang." Kyle punched another key. "This is phone tracking software. It can take some time, but it works. All we have to do is wait for…ah, bingo."

A map spread across the screen. A tiny green dot sat blinking on the edge of the River Thames, right where the Battersea power station used to be.

I frowned. "So, that's us, but where's the phone?"

Kyle pursed his lips. Balor growled.

And suddenly, I understood. That dot wasn't there to represent our location on the map at all. It represented the phone.

The killer was inside the Court.

24

"The killer is inside the Court?" I stared dumbly at the blinking green dot. "Like, right now?"

"Yes, that's how this works, Clark," Kyle said. I could tell he was giving me a hard time, but I didn't care. The killer was inside of this Court. That could only mean one thing.

I closed my eyes and took a step back, almost wishing I could rewind to the moment before I learned the truth. "Tiarnan. He's in the healing ward. This whole time I thought he was trying to track down the killer, but maybe I was wrong. I stopped by to see him last night. He definitely had a cell phone."

A moment passed in silence before the command room erupted into activity.

"Duncan, Moira. Come with me." Balor shouted the order, and his guards grabbed their weapons from the wall. Despite the fact that he'd completely ignored me, I wrapped my hand around the hilt of my sword and followed after them.

He stopped short when he realised I was behind him, but he didn't turn. It stung that he still refused to look me in the eye. "Stay here, Clark. You're not needed."

"If Tiarnan is involved in these murders, then I want to be there when you confront him about it. I could be useful. I can listen to his thoughts when he reacts."

"I thought you didn't want to be used for your mind reading powers," he said coolly. "I'm merely respecting the wishes you made very, very clear."

Ugh. I should have known he'd be in a mood.

"Look, just let me come, okay? It's not like we're leaving the Court."

"Fine." Balor turned toward Moira. "Keep an eye on her. If she gets in the way, take her out of there."

Moira pressed her lips together and nodded before shooting me a quick apologetic look. Without another word, Balor pushed through the door and led the way to the healing ward. We were silent as we approached Tiarnan's room. The nurses glanced up from down the hall, both with expressions of shock. Tiarnan had probably won them over. Just like he'd done with me.

Damn him.

But when we pushed into his room…his bed was empty.

"He's not here," Balor said in a low growl, and his hands curled into trembling fists. "Where the hell is he?"

"Master." Deirdre popped into the room, wringing her hands. "Is there a problem?"

"Tiarnan, the fae you have been healing," he said, jabbing a finger at the empty bed. "He's gone."

"Yes." She frowned, shot a panicked glance my way. "I didn't know he wasn't supposed to leave. He woke up fully healed this morning, so we let him go. I saw no reason to stop him."

"He left this morning," Balor repeated. "What time?"

"Er…" The nurse continued to wring her hands. "I believe it was just after six. I know it must have been around then because he didn't want to stay for breakfast, and we usually serve that at seven."

"Just after six." Balor sighed and swivelled toward Duncan. "He's not the one we're looking for. It isn't him. It's someone else."

"Wait." I forced myself to speak around the jolting beat of my heart. "What do you mean it isn't him?"

"The killer was inside this Court within the past ten minutes. Tiarnan left hours ago." He turned back toward the nurse. "Unless he left behind his phone?"

She quickly shook her head. "No, I went ahead and did a full clean of his room after he left. He didn't leave anything behind. No clothes. No phone. No nothing."

"It's someone else then," Balor said in that quiet, menacing voice of his. "And something has become very clear, something I should have realised weeks ago. The killer is someone who calls this Court his home."

⁂

We all stood in the Throne Room. Balor lounged on his throne of crimson skulls while the rest of his House stood at attention. The guards and I flanked him. Moira, Cormac, and

Duncan were on his left while Elise, Kyle, and I stood on the right. As soon as we'd confirmed the killer was still very much inside of this building by checking the tracking software one more time, Balor had called an assembly immediately.

Every single fae of House Beimnech now stood before us. All two hundred of them. Their expressions ranged from curiosity to unease to outright fear. They knew that the fae of this House had been going missing these past few weeks. They were likely scared. Unfortunately, their fear was about to get a hell of a lot worse. Balor had yet to announce that we'd found Rosalind and Abby, and he'd decided that today was the perfect opportunity to tell the House exactly what was going on.

And for me to listen in on their thoughts.

One of the fae standing before us now was the killer, and it was my job to pick him out of the crowd.

No pressure.

"Thank you all for coming," Balor said, his voice booming against the high stone walls. "I'm sure you're wondering why I called you here this morning. Unfortunately, I have some bad news."

A murmur went through the crowd, and Balor held up a hand to silence them.

"My team has been working diligently these past few weeks to find the person—fae or otherwise—responsible for taking Rosalind, Abby, Ondine, and now Lesley."

Gasps peppered the air. The fae shifted on their feet uneasily, casting worried glances at each other. Lesley's disappearance had been another detail Balor had chosen to keep quiet, momentarily. Now, it was all

LIVE FAE OR DIE TRYING

coming out. As much as he wanted to calm the Court's fears, shining light on the problem might be the only thing that could single out the killer. Balor hoped that discussing the disappearances would make the culprit think about his crimes, making it much easier for me to find him.

So, that was my cue to start listening in.

At first, I went slowly. There were hundreds of fae in this room. Some of their minds were sharper than others. They would take a little more plodding, a little more coaxing. Not to mention the fact that this was a *lot* of voices for me to manage at once. If I didn't take this slowly and carefully, their words could overwhelm me and drive me to my knees.

And honestly, I couldn't take the embarrassment. I'd already teetered around in front of these fae in too-tight heels. I kind of wanted to be the badass for once. The girl who had it all together. The take-charge member of the guard team who lifted her chin and pointed out the culprit, head held high.

Clark Cavanaugh, the half-fae who saved the day.

Anyway, I was getting a little carried away there. I'd never become the hero of my own story if I spent all my time daydreaming up scenarios that would never come true. Time to focus on the thoughts.

Deep breath in and out. Now, it was go time. When I first began to open my mind, words and thoughts came screaming toward me.

I can't believe Lesley is missing, too.
We're all doomed.
Why isn't Balor saving us?
Someone help us!
What is that new fae doing standing beside Balor's throne?

We need Fionn!
Help!

I squeezed my eyes shut, my chest heaving from the onslaught of thoughts and words and shouts and roars. There were too many of them, and they were all super emotional. This was going to be a hell of a lot trickier than I'd hoped.

"It is important that you all understand the gravity of the situation," Balor continued, seemingly oblivious to my struggle. "Rosalind and Abby were found two nights ago. They did not make it."

The voices screamed, louder and louder and louder. I gritted my teeth and tried to force my own mind to focus through the noise. There were so many thoughts, so much emotion. Their voices were charged, desperate, and angry.

We're all going to die.
Balor let them die.
I'm next.
I hate this Court!
HELP!?

My head swam. For a moment, I cut the voices off, snapping my mind away from them. I opened my eyes and peered blearily at the ground. Several of the fae standing at the edges of the carpet were staring at me and murmuring amongst themselves. They must have seen the way my face looked, they must have realised what I was doing.

I swayed a little on my feet.

Elise frowned and elbowed me in my side, shooting me a silent question mark.

I gave her a weak smile and a thumbs up, and then turned my attention back on the crowd. Regardless of how I felt, I had to keep going. We needed to find the killer. This was our only shot. Ondine and Lesley didn't have much time, and I had sworn that I would do whatever it took to find them.

The fae who stood before me were scared. They depended on the guards, on *us*, to keep them safe. And we were failing them. This wasn't just about Ondine anymore. It was about all of them. There were two hundred fae here. So many lives were at stake. I had to prevent the killer from targeting anyone else.

Balor held up a hand and stood. "I understand your fear, but you must trust me. I have been working closely with my guards, and we have been doing everything we can to put a stop to this. And to bring Ondine and Lesley home safe and sound."

No one argued, not with their Master and their Prince, but I could see the doubt painted on every single one of their faces. And, unfortunately, Balor was about to drop another bombshell right on top of their heads.

"During our investigation, we have discovered a very important, and very troublesome, bit of information." Balor's eye sparked, and then he glanced at me before continuing. This was it. The moment I'd been waiting for. I steeled my mind, held my breath, and waited. "We have tracked down the killer's location. To one building. This one. He is among us now. The killer is one of us." A long, strained pause followed while he took a deep breath in through his flared nostrils. "The House will be on lockdown until we determine who it is."

The Throne Room exploded into chaos. Everyone was screaming. Some out loud, some in their minds. I couldn't tell which was which, my own thoughts raging against the onslaught of unbridled emotion.

But despite the horror, I forced myself to focus. Thoughts flew at me as I picked my way through the crowd. Guttural screams smacked me in the face; hysterical tears tried to drag me down. I gritted my teeth and ignored the buzzing sensation that had begun to wrap its way around my body.

I had to find the killer. I had to stop him from hurting anyone else.

Wave after wave of thoughts flew over me as I continued to push my mind in a circle through the crowd. I dug in deep, pressing harder and harder against their minds. Slowly, the world began to fade.

The Throne Room became a distant memory the deeper I got into their minds. I got past the cries and the fear and the alarm and found myself in the very emotions that made them who they were.

Love, jealousy…happiness. Fear, hope, doubt.

Soon, I couldn't remember why I had come here anymore. Where was I? Who was I? There were so many voices that I couldn't pick out my own.

"Balor, something is wrong," I heard a voice say. It was so very far away. So distant that it must have been some other Earth in some other universe. She sounded as though she were deep inside a tunnel, one she could never escape.

"Clark?" A deep voice growled, and a strange magic skittered along my skin. Something shook me, and for a moment, my mind snapped high into the air. I looked down on a crowd from above, upon dozens of fae that were standing around, acting much calmer than they sounded in their minds. I'd expected a swarm of stomping, fleeing fae. Instead, they were wringing their hands and staring at a female fae plastered on the ground.

Wait.

Long red hair, pale face.

That female was me.

"Clark, come back to me," he said. I heard it both in my head and from his lips. He slid his arms underneath my body and lifted me from the ground. "I have to get her out of here. She's tried to do to much. Dammit, I shouldn't have asked her to try to read so many minds at once."

A hush fell across the crowd when Balor turned toward his Court with the redhead dangling in his arms. I snapped back into my body in an instant. My skull throbbed. My eyes felt as if they'd been ripped apart. But I felt safe. Balor held me close and strode out of the Throne Room, leaving behind every hope we had of finding the killer.

25

When I woke up, I sucked in a strangled breath when I realised that I wasn't in my bed. The sheets were dark and silky, unlike the white cotton of my own. Of course, maybe I was too delirious to understand what was happening. My skull still throbbed like I'd been stabbed with a seriously sharp pencil a hundred times.

Groaning, I twisted sideways to see that night had fallen. The tops of London's buildings rushed up to meet the sky, lights glittering from hundreds of windows. Out of the corner of my eye, a shadow moved.

I almost screamed.

Especially when I realised that shadow was Balor.

Oh my god, I *really* wasn't in my bed, was I? I was in his. In Balor's bed. Holy shit, I was in Balor's bed. My heart thrummed, and my entire body went tight.

He strode over to me, his expression hooded. I fidgeted with the covers, quickly giving myself a little check. I definitely didn't have any shoes on, but my clothes were all still in place. So, that meant he'd taken off my boots but not my shirt or my trousers.

I was a little more disappointed by that than I wanted to admit.

"Hello, Clark," he murmured, staring down at me. His voice alone made me shiver. "How are you feeling?"

"Like total shite," I answered honestly before reaching up to pat my head. "Did I fall and crack my skull or something?"

"You fell," he said, "but no, you didn't crack your skull. You may have damaged your mind though, at least temporarily."

Memories flooded into me then. Of all the voices, of all the screams. Instead of pulling back when things got dicey, I'd gone deeper into their minds. To be honest, it had been a pretty dumb move, but I'd been so determined to find the killer that my own well-being hadn't mattered at the time.

"So, you're telling me I collapsed in front of the entire House?"

"I'm afraid so," he said. "They're all very worried about you. Moira and Elise, especially. They tried to insist on following us up here, but I thought you might need a break from other people's thoughts for awhile. It seemed like you lost the control to shut them out. I wasn't sure if your mind could take even a single person's presence right now. Except for mine, of course."

Right. So that explained why he brought me here instead of taking me straight to the healing ward. He knew that he could keep his thoughts hidden from me when others couldn't. Balor's mind was blissfully silent. Something I never thought I'd say.

And, as much as I hated to admit it, he'd been right.

"It's happened before," I admitted. "The loss of control thing, I mean. Not a lot. Only a few times. Normally, I don't let things get that bad. But once it gets to that point, there's no stopping it. I opened my mind too wide, and I couldn't close it back down again. I should be okay now though."

"You don't look okay, Clark."

"I'm fine." I pushed myself up higher on the pillows, wincing at another sudden throb in my head. "A little wobbly, but fine. I need to get back to the mission. There must be something else we can do."

"You need to rest," Balor said with a frown. "The team is currently handling the situation, going through every room to find evidence, taking every single phone. Kyle will be able to match it to the device he tracked."

I shook my head, my red hair falling around my face. "You won't be able to find evidence."

"Why?" Balor's voice went sharp. "Did you hear something?"

"No, that's just it," I said softly. "I didn't hear a damn thing. I don't think the killer was in that room, Balor."

Balor frowned and turned away. "What are you talking about? Of course he was in that room. We tracked the phone. Every fae in the House was there. Duncan and Cormac made certain of it."

"I don't understand how it happened, but he wasn't in there. I didn't even hear a hint of him."

Balor stalked over to his floor-to-ceiling window, with its glittering view of London's streets. He curled his hands into fists. They shook by his sides until he braced them against the glass. "Surely you were not able to listen to every mind in that room. There were hundreds in there. You lost control of your power. You collapsed."

"I know you don't want to believe me," I said, pushing up from the pillows so that I could swing my legs over the side of the bed. With a deep breath, I stood and strode over to his side. My legs were shaky, but they were strong. "To be honest, I don't want to believe it either. It would be a hell of a lot easier on us all if the killer was in that room, if it was only a matter of finding the right phone to match it to the right fae."

He turned toward me then, his jaw rippling. "And you're telling me it's not that easy."

"I'm afraid not." I peered up at him, sighing when I saw the doubt in his eye. I might not be able to read his mind, but I was quickly starting to understand him in ways I'd never understood anyone else. That look on his face right there. It was the hope that I was wrong.

"The reason I collapsed is because I did too much. I scanned the entire room. I went from mind to mind, putting myself out there to each and every one of them. The sound was like a cacophony of screams and fear and pain." I sucked in a sharp breath and stared out at the twinkling lights. "But *because* it was like that, I know that I would have heard the one single voice that stood out from the rest. If there'd been a fae in the room thinking insane murderous thoughts, I would have heard him. He would have sounded different. He would have been the total opposite of fear."

Balor scowled. It wasn't what he wanted to hear, and I couldn't blame him.

"If he wasn't in there, then where the hell was he?" he demanded.

I lifted my shoulders in a shrug. "I don't know, Balor. Maybe he heard about the assembly and ran off. Maybe he somehow knows about my power and figured out what we had planned."

"Every single fae who lives in this House attended the meeting this morning," Balor said, narrowing his eye. "Names were checked off. It was confirmed."

"I…" I lifted my hands and shook my head. We had tried a lot by this point. We'd searched the House. We'd poked into every House Beimnech fae's head. We had spied on and confronted Fionn. There weren't many options left. At this point, the culprit was probably long gone. We hadn't played our cards close enough to our chest. He'd been here, only hours earlier, but then we'd scared him off. The only way to find him would be…

"Maybe we should set a trap for him," I said.

Balor shifted toward me, eyebrow raised. "A trap? Explain."

"Well, I was just thinking that we've obviously scared him off. If we want to find him, we need to *un*-scare him off."

Balor's lips twitched. "I don't think 'un-scare' is a word, but go on."

I rolled my eyes at him. "Anyway, how do we do that? By luring him back in. With a trap. We need to set up a situation where an unsuspecting brunette is alone and unarmed and too tempting to resist."

"You want me to use one of my fae as bait."

"Basically? Yes." The idea started gaining steam in my mind, so I plowed forward. "Whoever it is, I don't think he went far. He's probably even watching the House, waiting to see what you do. Now you just need a brunette fae to pretend to break out of lockdown and head to your club. Maybe she decides to step out into the alley for a smoke while she's there. Alone."

Balor slowly nodded his head. "I see where you're going with this." He scowled. "And I don't like it. It puts another one of my fae in danger. They've been through enough."

"She would be protected. You and all of us guards could be close by."

"Hmm." I could tell that my idea had sparked some hope in him, but he didn't want to admit it.

As we'd begun to talk, he'd drifted a little further away. His expression had been concerned when I'd first woken up, but he was shutting himself off to me now that he could see I was clearly okay.

He was probably still pissed off about what I'd said. And, even though I'd meant every word, I probably could have handled things a teensy bit better.

I sighed, leaned my forehead against the cool glass. "Balor."

"Yes?" He twisted toward me, eyebrow winging upward.

"Listen. About last night."

He held up a hand and shook his head. "Don't."

"I said a lot of things I probably shouldn't have," I said, nibbling on my bottom lip. My gaze stayed focused on the street-lamps that lined the pavement down below. "I guess I just wanted to say sorry. It's obviously none of my business who you sleep with."

It pained me to say that, even though it was the truth.

"You're right," he said. "It isn't any of your business. And I don't appreciate some of the accusations you hurled at me."

I blew out a hot breath. "Like I said, I'm sorry."

Did that mean I wasn't still curious about why he didn't bring girls back here? Damn straight I was. But it had nothing to do with Ondine or Lesley, and I needed to keep my focus on what mattered.

Balor Beimnech's lips? They didn't matter.

"Hmm." Balor edged closer, strategically shifting his body in between mine and the window. "I'll admit, I didn't expect you to apologise. You're very stubborn, Clark."

"Sometimes people can surprise you." And I wasn't sure if I was referring to myself or to him.

"Yes, they can." He lifted a finger to my face but didn't touch me, his magic curling gently across my cheek. "You scared me, Clark. In the Throne Room. You looked…gone. I wasn't sure if I'd be able to save you."

"I'm tougher than I look." My voice came out a whisper, and I desperately tried not to lean into his touch. But that was impossible. My body answered to his, my soul called out for more. Closing my eyes, I shifted toward him, pressing my cheek against his open palm.

When we touched, magic sparked along my skin. That deep, dark fire I'd thought we had doused came roaring back to life. That power filled every single inch of me, pulling my body up against my Master's until there was nothing left but a breath of nothingness between us.

"Clark," Balor growled, shuddering at the desire I knew we both felt. He shook his head, his eye flashing with a combination of need, of pain, of fear. "The kiss we shared. It was a mistake. We cannot do this."

"Why?" I demanded, even though I knew the answer to that question for myself. There were a million reasons why I should run—fast—away from this. But that didn't mean I wanted to. Logic was nothing compared to how my body felt when he was near.

"I am not good for you." He placed his hands on my shoulders and gently pushed me back. "And you are not good for me. We can never give in to this, Clark. *Never*. It was a mistake to bring you to my room. You should go."

I blinked at him, desperately trying to hold back the tears. His words hurt far more than they should. He was only voicing a truth I knew deep down inside.

So, I grabbed my boots and turned to go.

"Wait," he said, voice rough.

My heart lifted as I glanced over my shoulder.

"You still have healing to do. Go straight to your room and stay there for the rest of the night." He tore his gaze away, placed an unsteady hand on the window. "That's an order from your Master."

"Yes," I whispered, and finally, a tear did splash onto my cheek. "My Master and nothing more."

26

Halfway back to my room, my burner phone buzzed in my pocket. Frowning, I glanced at the screen, and a strange storm of emotions tore through me. The text was from Tiarnan. This was his last night in London. He'd found some information he thought I needed to know. And…here was the kicker, he wanted to see me.

Sighing, I slid the phone into my pocket and leaned heavily against the wall. A few fae passed me by in the corridor, giving me funny looks. Eh, whatever. Let them stare.

Tiarnan had some information. Tiarnan also wanted to see me.

I didn't know how I felt about the second part of that equation. Sure, we'd kind of bonded in a way. And sure, he was an attractive warrior. And nice.

He was the opposite of Balor Beimnech.

Which meant…he wasn't anything like Balor at all.

Besides, Balor's orders had been pretty specific. He

wanted me to go back to my room and get some rest. Right now, the team was searching every room of this House, hoping to find evidence that would point to the killer.

But I was pretty certain they were looking in the wrong place. I'd heard nothing from the fae in the Throne Room, which meant the killer was out on London's streets and not in this House. And it sounded like Tiarnan knew something about it.

Pursing my lips, I decided to send my own text: *What kind of information?*

A minute later, I got my answer.

It's about the killer. I found some evidence, and I think I know who it is. Will you meet me?

I drummed my fingers against my thigh, nibbling on my bottom lip. I probably shouldn't go. For one, Balor's wishes had been clear. And second? Well, if I was being honest, I was feeling kind of raw. I'd just been rejected. By a fae I shouldn't even want in the first place.

I kind of just wanted to mope. But…this could be important. Two fae lives hung in the balance. If there was something I could do to help, I needed to do it. Damn the consequences.

Okay. When and where?
Temple Pier. One hour.

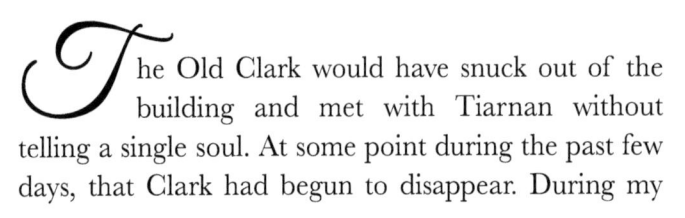

~

The Old Clark would have snuck out of the building and met with Tiarnan without telling a single soul. At some point during the past few days, that Clark had begun to disappear. During my time at the Crimson Court, I'd learned that, hey, sometimes it's better to talk to people about what's going on.

So, that's what I did.

After changing into a fresh pair of black guard clothes and splashing water onto my face, I went downstairs to check on things in the command station. Things were...well, crazy was really the only word I could use to accurately describe it. The place had descended into chaos. Court members were streaming in and out, dumping boxes onto folding tables that had been erected in the middle of the room. Everyone was grumbling. And a lot of people looked scared. Elise's eyes were wild; Cormac was storming about with a scowl plastered to his face.

"Hey, Kyle," I said, easing up to his side. He was taking refuge at his computer station, hunkered down and tapping away at a blank screen. Clearly pretending to work to avoid this insanity. I couldn't blame him. He had a stack of cell phones on the desk beside him, but they'd each been cleared, a green post-it note stuck on the top.

"This is awful. I don't like being around so many people."

"I hear you." I gave his shoulder a quick pat. "Listen, where's Moira? Or Duncan? Also, have you seen Balor in the past fifteen minutes? He's not in his room."

I had actually checked, a fact that I was pretty proud of. Instead of racing off into the night without giving him a heads up, I had gone back to his penthouse to tell him about the text I'd gotten from Tiarnan. But he hadn't been there.

"Oh. You didn't hear?" Kyle shot a nervous smile over his shoulder. "They all went out to try and trap the killer."

What?!

"They did?" I...actually couldn't believe it. That meant that Balor had actually listened to me. When I'd first brought up my whole trap-the-killer idea, he'd been so dismissive.

But he'd actually decided to go through with it. All because of...well, me.

Huh.

And yet, he hadn't taken me with him. He hadn't even told me. Instead, he'd rejected me and taken his other guards with him instead. I didn't want to be a baby about it, but I wasn't a robot. It kind of hurt.

"Thanks, Kyle." I pushed away from the computer station and strode over to Elise. She whirled this way and that, her usually smooth silver hair piled on top of her head in a messy bun. With a clipboard in her hands, she spun to face me. She took in my outfit, shook her head.

"You're supposed to be resting. Balor's orders," she chirped before turning toward a new cluster of fae who had come to ask when they'd be getting back their phones.

Elise was busy. Kyle just wanted to be left alone.

I found myself drifting out the door.

"Good." Elise spotted me heading through the archway and gave me a thumbs up. "*Go rest.*"

But I wasn't going to rest. I was going to find out what Tiarnan knew, so we could track this killer down. Balor was out there trying to trap him. And I needed to help.

LIVE FAE OR DIE TRYING

My footsteps echoed on the hard pavement as I strolled along the River Thames toward Temple. The moon hung low in the sky, hidden behind the jutting rooftops of London buildings. A heavy fog had settled in on the ground, a wintry mist that shrouded the world in a haze of white.

On my way to Temple, I tried to ring Balor, but the line went straight to voicemail. Frowning, I pocketed my phone and shrugged my hands into the slim pockets of my leather jacket. He was obviously busy with his new mission. The one he hadn't even bothered to tell me about, even though it had been my idea.

Trap the killer.

Would it work? I hoped so. If not, the information from Tiarnan could prove invaluable.

I rested my hand on the hilt of my sword as I got closer to the pier. Because *yes.* Of course I brought my weapon. I might act a little rashly sometimes, but I'd learned my lesson. Never go anywhere without a weapon, even if I'd only just begun to learn how to use it.

My feet slowed as I reached the pier. By itself, the pier was fairly nondescript. There was a set of steps leading up to a concrete block that jutted out over the water. Often, boats would be docked here. Party boats, normally. At the moment, there was nothing. Nothing but the lazy current drifting by.

I blew hot breath onto my chilly hands and whirled in a slow circle. It had taken me just about an hour to walk here from the Court, so I was pretty much right on time. Tiarnan had said an hour, right?

Just to be sure, I checked my phone. Yep, he'd said an hour.

Unease flickered in my gut as I slid my phone back into my pocket. Maybe he was late. Of course, the last time I'd been on my way to meet someone and they'd been late, a mysterious fae had knocked me out.

At the memory, my heartbeat sped up. With all the excitement of the past few days, I'd almost forgotten about that strange attack in the middle of the London streets. I'd pretty much confirmed, at least in my heart, that Balor wasn't the fae behind the attack.

So, it must have been the killer.

And now, I was standing alone on the nighttime streets, waiting to meet someone who hadn't yet showed. Again.

Only this time, no humans bustled by. There were no cabs zooming down the streets. The street-lamps were even dark. Sucking in a deep breath, I glanced up. They'd been smashed.

"Shit," I whispered, holding tight to my sword's hilt.

The killer had lured me here. I knew it deep down in my bones. Here I'd thought that I'd been the smart one, telling Balor to do the luring himself. Instead, the killer had been two steps ahead of us. Again.

I needed to get out of here, get back to the Court.

Keeping my eyes cast to the ground, I slowly turned back the way I'd come and hurried down the pavement. I only made it five steps before a body hurtled into my way. I stumbled back, heart revolting in my chest.

It was the same fae who had attacked me before. The dark mask, the hidden face, the tall, lithe body that moved impossibly fast. Well, kind of tall. Taller than me but still too small to be Tiarnan. Way too small to be Balor.

No, this was someone else.

I pulled my sword from the sheath and held it before me, just like Moira had taught me. In my wildest dreams, the attacker would see my badass weaponry, turn tail, and run.

The killer didn't do that, of course.

She laughed.

Yep, *she*. Her laugh was light and delicate, but it definitely had a massive dose of evil. Like a cackle. I narrowed my eyes and tightened my grip on the hilt, her laughter carrying across the pier.

"You can laugh all you want, but that's not going to stop me from slicing through your armpit."

I had no idea why I said that. It seemed like a good idea at the time. No one would want a sword cutting through their armpit. It would hurt like hell, *and* your arm would fall off.

That said, it was definitely one of those things that sounded a hell of a lot better in my head.

"You are such a disease. Filthy Carrion," she hissed. Magic rippled from her body and onto mine, a skittering kind of darkness that made every hair on my arm wish it could just jump right off my body and run.

"Nice one," I snarked. "You kiss your mum with that mouth?"

All I had to do was keep this fae talking, and then I would somehow do something I hadn't yet thought of, and that special, amazing, perfect idea would lead to my escape. *Think, Clark. Think.*

"You don't know how to use that thing," she said, sneering and dancing a step closer. I jumped back.

"I know that if I shove the sharp thingy in your direction, then you won't be able to kill any more fae."

She laughed again. "You think you're clever, but you have no idea what this world is like."

"Oh yeah?" I arched a brow. "Then tell me what it's like."

New plan. This fae was clearly bonkers. Instead of running, I needed to keep her talking so that I could find out who she was and what she had planned. All it would take was a small dip into her mind. I'd have to concentrate though, especially after I overdid it in the Throne Room. Tricky, since I was also holding a sword.

"Balor Beimnech is a traitor to Faerie."

Ah, that old chestnut again.

"You sound a hell of a lot like Fionn. Are you in his Court?"

She laughed again, a little louder, a little less sane. Shaking her head, she inched closer. I took a step back, keeping my sword held before me.

"You have no idea who I am, do you?" She laughed again. "I should have known. You've been so self-involved, so obsessed with Balor Beimnech that you didn't even notice anything about me." Her voice dropped; her accent went flat. Flat like mine. "Know who I am now?"

"Wait." Blood rushed into my cheeks. She was right. I *had* heard her voice before. Only a few times, but— "*Lesley?*"

"Surprise!" She held up her hands—which were very much not gloved for once—and laughed again. She really was a fan of laughing, and it was creeping me the fuck out.

"But…" I shook my head, not understanding. "We thought you were missing. We've been looking for you. How are you the one who's behind this? Why would you kill other faeries?"

Lesley's laugh died. She went silent, her two dark eyes flashing through the mask. Curious, I reached out, desperate to understand her motive. She was one of the guards. She'd been a trusted member of the team. Balor had taken her into his Court. He had given her everything she needed and more.

Why had she done this?

What an idiot. She's reading my mind when I'm two seconds away from stopping her heart. All I have to do is touch her.

And then everything went black.

27

I pried open my eyes to see a grimy wall. Musty clouds swirled into my nose, and a small nearby flashlight was the only thing illuminating the metal bars that surrounded me. Frowning, I pushed up from the floor and gazed around. I was in some kind of a tunnel. A few moments passed as I squinted my eyes, vision adjusting to the darkness.

After a few moments, shapes became clearer. I was definitely in a tunnel, but more than that? It looked like a tube stop. Rusted old train tracks disappeared into darkness, the domed ceiling curving high above. To my right, I noticed black letters that spelled out the word *Aldwych*. We were in the old abandoned tube station, the one shut down after it became a bomb shelter during the war.

"You're awake," a male voice said from behind me.

I screamed. Like, actually screamed. It was a loud one, too, echoing off the walls.

Curling my hands into fists, I scuttled back and

faced the owner of said voice. And then all the fight went out of me at once.

"Tiarnan?"

He looked bad. Really bad. Way worse than I felt and that was saying something. My head felt as though it had been split in two, and my chest ached from whatever Lesley had done to me.

She stopped my heart.

Tiarnan peered up at me, dirt caked to his skin, purple bags underneath his eyes. It had only been a day or so since I'd seen him, but he looked as though he'd been trapped in this tube station for years.

"What's going on?" I dropped to my knees, pressed the hair out of his eyes. "What has she done to you?"

He coughed, lungs rattling. "Trying to get information out of me. She's stopped my heart about a hundred times."

All the blood drained from my face. "How are you….how are you even alive?"

"Luckily, I'm fae and I heal. Plus, the Fianna magic is strong," he whispered. "I don't know how many more times I can take it though. She wore me down, Clark. I gave her what she wanted. I'm so sorry."

"What do you mean?" I asked quietly.

"I told her how to get to Fionn. Once she destroys your House, she's going to destroy mine. Until there is not a single fae left of the Crimson Court who is loyal to Balor Beimnech. She wants a revolt. And honestly, I think she's going to get it."

My blood roared in my veins, and unshed tears burned my eyes. How was she doing this? And why?

From somewhere in the distance, a scuttling sound met my ears. I stiffened, sucking in a sharp breath. I reached for my sword, but it was gone.

"You think I would have let you keep your weapon? That would have made me such a dumbass." Lesley laughed as she slid into view. She stood halfway down the platform, twirling a dagger in her open palm. Now, she no longer wore her mask. Her long dark hair hung around her shoulders in loose waves, and her tiny, sharp nose was like a dagger in the dark. When I'd first met her, I'd noticed how slight she was, and I'd wondered why she was a member of the guard.

Things were starting to make a little more sense. Kind of.

"I don't understand what's happening. What are you doing, Lesley?" I pushed up against the bars of the metal cage. "What's the whole point of this? Why do you want to destroy the Court?"

"Ah." She shot me a smile full of teeth. "I see that your little pet has been blabbing to you."

My *pet*? I wrinkled my nose.

With a roll of her eyes, she began to pace from one end of the tube station to the other, passing close to the edge of the platform that led down to the tracks. "If you hadn't spent most of your life as a Courtless fae, you'd understand why I'm taking him down. Hell, you'd probably want to help me. You seem like the kind of fae who has a mind of her own. And he does *not* like fae who have minds of their own. Except you, strangely."

"Take down who?"

"Balor Beimnech." She stopped her pacing and

laughed that demented laugh of hers again. I really wished she'd stop doing that. "He doesn't deserve to be Prince."

So, this whole thing had to do with Balor. Honestly, I wasn't all that surprised. While he seemed to inspire devout devotion in some, he also seemed to generate some pretty seething hatred from others. Maybe he was like marmite. You either loved him or you hated him, but you couldn't just *kind of* be into him.

"Interesting." I tried to keep my voice nonchalant as I wrapped my hands around the metal bars of my cage. "I'm guessing you and Fionn get along well then. He also doesn't think Balor deserves to be the Prince. In fact, I hear he has plans pretty similar to yours. Maybe because you've been working together?"

She snorted, rolling her eyes again. "You've got to be kidding me. Fionn is what the British like to call a wanker, including every single one of his Fianna." She gave a pointed look in Tiarnan's direction.

I glanced toward the warrior. His eyes had slid shut during my conversation with Lesley. He was clearly at the end of his rope, too worn down to even keep his eyes open. Would that be me in twenty-four hours? After having my heart stopped a hundred times? Truth be told, I probably wouldn't even make it that long. I didn't have Tiarnan's strength. My blood wasn't one-hundred percent fae.

She had obviously brought me down here to kill me. Gritting my teeth, I strengthened my resolve. Well, she could damn well try, but I wasn't going down without a fight.

"I guess I'm confused. If you aren't with Fionn,

then who are you with?" I said, turning my attention back her way. She'd plopped down on the wooden bench, glancing at her watch every now and again. What was she waiting for?

She glanced up. "I'm with no one, at least not while I'm here on foreign soil." She sighed when I continued to give her a blank look. "Nemain sent me. She wanted me to infiltrate the Crimson Court since Balor is only going to end up destroying it. His alliances with vamps and shifters? Not gonna happen."

"Right," I said slowly. "So, let me get this straight. You came over here from America on the order of your Princess."

"My *Queen*," she corrected. "The future Queen of all of Faerie."

"Anyway," I said, holding back the urge to roll my eyes. "She wanted you to tear apart his Court, so you decided to…murder some of his fae? And put them in white dresses in the catacombs? Why wouldn't you just kill him instead? Help me out here, Lesley. It's not quite adding up together in my head."

"Listen, Courtless," she said. "Balor Beimnech is not that easy to take out. Kill him and he becomes a martyr for his people. We can't have that."

Realisation dawned. "You were trying to frame him."

"Bingo!" She clapped and stood. "Finally, you get it. I took two brunette fae, the kind he likes, and then I left them in the catacombs for Fionn to find. He was supposed to accuse Balor after that."

Slowly, I nodded. "You were the anonymous tip."

"Exactly." She strode up close to the bars to peer

in at me. "I figured if people thought he was murdering his own fae, then the House would fall apart. It was easy to cover up, being a guard. All it took was a little tampering of the security footage, and that was that. Unfortunately, you've made things very difficult for me. You keep sticking your nose in, messing things up. Everyone knows it wasn't Balor at this point, so I've had to pivot. That's where you come in."

Lovely. My heart skipped a beat.

"Mind sharing what you mean by that?" I asked as nonchalantly as I could.

She stepped up to the bars, and her smile went wide. "I know what Balor is up to this evening. He and his idiot guards are trying to set a trap for the 'serial killer' taking his fae. They're trying to lure me out with the temptation of a lonely brunette, like I'm somehow going to see her and find the whole thing far too irresistible. What he doesn't know is that it was never about the girls. It was about him. So, I've set my own trap in return. *You.*"

Shit. I wet my lips and shook my head. "Well, that's where you're going to fail. Balor doesn't care about me. You picked the wrong fae to use as bait."

Although maybe I shouldn't have said that. I didn't want her to go find yet another fae to knock out. I didn't want her to stop someone else's heart, too.

Lesley laughed, the sound echoing through the tunnel. "You can lie all you want, but I know the truth. I was there, Clark, at the Court when he brought you around, showing you off like his new prize. He has taken a liking to you. He will come."

"Why set a trap though?" I asked quickly,

desperate to keep her talking. If I did, she might not have a chance to lure Balor here before morning. "If you don't want to make him a martyr, then you're right. Killing him isn't in the plan."

"Yeah, but plans change," she said with a wave of her hand. "I have a new plan now. I'm going to set a scene, like in a film. What do you think of this? Tiarnan here was trying to kill you on Fionn's orders, in order to frame Balor for your death. Balor finds out about it, comes to save the day, but he ends up dying to protect you. You die in the crossfire, of course." She laughed again. "It's insane enough that it will tear the Court to shreds, giving Nemain the perfect opportunity to step in and take over. Easy. Peasy."

Didn't sound particularly easy peasy to me. It sounded fucking insane.

She glanced at her watch, and her eyes lit up. "Ah, it's time. Clark, I need you to call Balor and tell him you're being held captive in the old Aldwych tube station."

I crossed my arms over my chest and lifted my chin. "Good luck with that."

"You refuse my orders?" She pursed her lips, tapped them with her long fingernail. "Can't say I'm surprised. That's alright. I brought something along just in case you needed some encouragement."

My heart thumped as she spun on her feet and disappeared into the darkness at the far end of the tunnel. Shadows enveloped her like a blanket. A moment later, she reappeared, one hand swinging by her side, the other wrapped tight around a handful of grimy black hair. She strode toward me with insane fire dancing in her eyes as she dragged a limp, waxen form behind her.

My heart leapt into my throat. I couldn't see the girl's face, but I knew who it was. I recognised the jacket; I knew those jeans. I remembered when she had asked me what I thought of them one night when we'd met near Big Ben.

Lesley had Ondine.

Ondine. My heart squeezed tight.

She was in bad shape, but she was still alive.

I almost dropped to my knees, but I clung on tight to the bars, refusing to let Lesley see just how much she'd gotten to me.

Suddenly, Lesley stopped. She let go of Ondine's hair, and her body slumped against the ground.

"Now," Lesley said. "I'm hoping that we understand each other a little better now. You're going to make that phone call to Balor, and you're going to tell him to come save you. Not a word about me and not a word about Tiarnan. Understood? You're here, you're trapped, and you're alone."

Swallowing hard, I nodded.

"I don't think I need to tell you that I will kill Ondine if you say anything I don't like," she said, lifting a brow. "But I'm telling you anyway. Do what I say, Clark. For once in your life, obey some fucking orders."

She strode over to the metal cage and shoved the phone through the bars. I took it with trembling hands, punched in Balor's number, and lifted the speaker to my ear. It rang twice, and then he answered.

"Clark?" His voice was panicked, deep, and full of

confusion. "Kyle said he saw you an hour ago and that you were acting weird, so I went to go check on you. You're not in your room. I'm trying not to jump to conclusions, but—"

"I've been taken," I said in a gasp, squeezing shut my eyes. I hated doing this to him. I hated speaking these words aloud. The last thing I wanted to do was lure Balor into a trap, but I didn't know what other choice I had. If I didn't follow Lesley's orders, Ondine would die. "The killer got me. I'm trapped in some kind of cage. In Aldwych station. Balor, please…I—"

The phone got ripped away from my ear. Bright light tore through the tunnel. And then everything went black again.

28

At some point, I woke up again. Lesley was nowhere to be seen. Neither was Ondine. Now that she'd gotten what she needed, she'd probably dragged Ondine back into the shadows. Lesley was no doubt lurking somewhere nearby, just waiting for Balor to save the day.

My heart hurt just thinking about it. If he died here tonight, I'd never be able to forgive myself for the phone call I'd made. I knew Lesley had given me no other choice, but that fact didn't help my guilt.

"And she's back," Tiarnan mumbled. "You're recovering faster than I am at this point, but you're only on your second time."

Frowning, I pushed myself up into a sitting position, leaning heavily against the rusted metal bars. "Let me guess. She stopped my heart again."

"Yes, and she'll do it again if you annoy her. Trust me. One time, I made a joke about her maniacal smile, and she zapped me."

"Her smile really is maniacal."

Sighing, I dropped my head back against the bars and stared up at the dark, domed ceiling. I'd spent my whole life on the run. I'd fought for my freedom every step of the way. I'd gotten scrappy, doing whatever it took to survive. Nothing had been able to get me down. Not fully.

No matter what had happened, no matter how broke I'd been, life had never felt impossible. I'd always had hope.

Until now.

We were freakin' doomed.

"I don't suppose you have a time machine?" I asked Tiarnan.

"Sure. Right here in my pocket next to the special armour that kills anyone who tries to stop my heart."

"Very useful," I said, a slight smile cresting my lips. "Although, it probably would have been a good idea to don that thing about ninety-nine heart stops ago."

"Ah, if only I'd thought of that myself." He dramatically pressed his hand to his heart. "You are so much smarter than me, Clark Cavanaugh. Maybe it's the shifter part of you."

The smile died from my lips. "Seriously though. Are you okay, Tiarnan? No offence, but you kind of look like shit."

"None taken. I feel exactly how I look. I'm feeling a bit better now that you're here though."

"Glad I could be of service. You did ignore my request though," I said. "Our first date was supposed to take place anywhere other than the underground. There may not be any Sluagh here, but I'm dead certain this counts as a dungeon."

"But Aldwych Station has such a romantic ambience. There's slime covering the walls, about a million rats building a nest over there, and don't forget the sociopathic murderess who will return any minute now."

I pressed my lips together, tension rippling through my cheeks. "She won't return until Balor gets here. She's using me as bait. And I'm pretty sure it's going to work."

Tiarnan's dark eyes met mine, and a spark appeared there, even if he was the most beat down he could possibly be. "You have to stop her, Clark. You cannot let her get away with this."

I blinked at him. "*Me?* What the hell am I supposed to do? If anyone is capable of stopping her, wouldn't it be the warrior who has spent his entire life training for battle? That's you last time I checked. Not me."

"If you haven't noticed, I'm kind of out of commission over here."

Kind of was putting it mildly. He could barely hold himself up.

I dropped my voice to a low whisper. Just because I couldn't see Lesley didn't mean she wasn't there. And I couldn't let her hear my next words.

"What can I possibly do to stop her?" I mouthed. "We're stuck in a cage, and she'll stop Ondine's heart if I make a wrong move."

Tiarnan reached out and placed a gentle hand against my cheek. My heart fluttered, something deep inside of me responding to his touch. "Honestly, Clark? I have no idea. But you're stronger and smarter than you think. I'm putting all my faith in you to get us out of here. Also, you owe me." He grinned. "I saved you from that Sluagh, remember?"

Damn him. Bringing up the whole Sluagh disaster when I'd barely been able to hold a sword. This time, things weren't much better. I didn't even have a sword now. Neither did Tiarnan. If we were going to survive this, my mind would have to do all the work.

Footsteps echoed through the underground. I jumped to my feet, heart jolting in my chest. Lesley whispered out of the darkness at the other end of the tunnel, her eyes bouncing with pure, overblown excitement.

There really was something wrong with that girl. This was more than just some mission to her. She delighted in the darkness, in the violence. That could come in handy if I played my cards right.

"Clark?" Balor's deep melodic voice rang out in the silence.

I opened my mouth to call to him, but Lesley held up a finger, shook her head, and sliced it right across her neck. Okay then. I backed up a bit, turning to see if Tiarnan had heard Balor's call. The poor guy had passed out again. I knew without a doubt that his heart was giving out. He probably didn't have much time until he was gone for good.

Determination roiled through me. I was only one fae. A half-fae at that. And totally new to the Court. But I had power. I could do things most other fae could not. And while I was probably going to end up dead from this night, I had to fight as hard as I could. I couldn't let Lesley win.

Balor stepped off of the stairs and onto the underground platform. My heart lifted, just at seeing him.

Power rippled from his body in waves, his shoulders thrown back as he scanned the tunnel. His single red eye landed on me, and he started, breath catching in his throat. So much passed between us in that instant. Desire, regret, need, and hope.

And a deep, deep fear that this would be the last time I would ever see my Prince alive.

"Balor, watch out!" I shouted just as Lesley inched up behind him. Power rushed through the tunnel like a storm, bright magic swirling around her fingers.

But it was too late. She placed her glowing hand on his bare arm. His eye opened wide as if he'd just seen a ghost. And then the most powerful fae I'd ever met tumbled to the ground.

29

*L*esley immediately got to work. She huffed and puffed as she dragged Balor's massive body toward a brick column in the center of the platform. A moment later, she disappeared and then came back carrying a heavy chain. She wrapped it around Balor's body, locking it tight when she was done.

"There," she said, brushing her hands together and looking more than a little bit pleased with herself. "He won't be going anywhere, and no way in hell he can remove his eye patch like that."

"Well done," I said dryly. "What exactly are you trying to accomplish with that? I thought you wanted to stage some kind of triple homicide between the three of us."

"And I'm going to do just that, don't you worry. I just need a little information from him first." She turned and pointed in my direction. "And you're going to get it for me."

"Me?"

"Don't play dumb," she said. "I know you're a mind reader. Balor announced it to the whole damn guard team. I might not have been there in person that day, but trust me, nothing happens in that room without me knowing about it."

Well, that was certainly interesting. Lesley didn't know that I couldn't read Balor's mind. No way in hell was I going to correct her either. She could just keep on thinking it as long as she wanted, because that meant we might have a chance.

All I needed to do was stall her, long enough to come up with a plan.

"Ah right. You caught me," I said, throwing up my hands in mock exasperation. "Damn. I didn't think you'd know about my power."

"Well, I do. Now, read his mind."

"Okay, there are just a couple of problems with what you're asking me to do. First, he's unconscious. I can't read someone's mind who isn't awake. Second, I have no idea what you want to know. If I try to read his mind without a map, so to speak, I'll just end up getting gibberish."

My heart beat so hard that I swore she'd be able to hear it from across the tunnel. It would give me away. I was lying through my teeth, and she would know it. She frowned as she stalked toward me, striding so close to the metal bars that I could smell whiskey rolling off her body in waves.

She was drunk. More than that. She was bloody pissed.

"Also," I said, "sometimes I find it difficult to use my powers when I'm tense. You have the same problem?"

Her eyes widened, and she gave a quick nod. "Actually, yes. It's totally the same for me. You know what helps? Booze. I have a bottle of Jack with me. Would you like a shot?"

Ding, dong, the witch was dead. Or she would be. Thanks to the magical elixir that was Jack Daniels. Words I *never* in a million years thought I'd say.

"I would love a shot. Thank you."

This was my ticket out of this cage. She couldn't give me a drink without opening the door.

Lesley hurried over to a rucksack she'd tossed in the corner. She dug through it, bottles clinking. After a few moments, she pulled a bottle of Jack from her bag. Only about a quarter of the amber liquid was left. It sloshed in the glass bottle as she strode back over.

"Now, listen. I'm going to share this with you because I need your powers to be at their best. I don't trust you though. So, I'm going to pour this into a shot glass and hand it to you through the bars."

Dammit. I hadn't counted on her having a damn shot glass. Who carries one around with them? It was absolutely ludicrous. And it meant that I now had no way to get out of this damn cage. *And* that I'd have to take the shot of Jack Daniels (*ugh!*), somehow keeping my wits about me long enough to win in a fight against this fae.

Lesley pulled a shot glass from her pocket—yes, her pocket—poured the drink, and then passed it to me. I tried to keep my expression neutral, but inwardly, I was revolting. But hey, I'd gotten myself into this mess. Time to put my big girl pants on, grin and bear it, and all that good stuff.

I tipped back my head and poured the liquid down my throat.

It burned. Oh god, it burned.

My eyes watered. My cheeks flamed.

With a tight smile, I passed the shot glass back to Lesley. She was watching me with eyebrows raised.

"I'm a gin and tonic kind of girl myself, so I'm not really used to taking shots." I punched my chest and coughed. "That sure was good though."

Lies, lies, lies. It was bloody horrendous.

"Good." She gave a nod. "Now what? Can you read his mind?"

"Calm yourself. This isn't something I can rush. He'll have to be conscious before I can read his mind," I said with a shrug. "Although I'm going to be totally honest with you, since you've just shared some booze with me. I find Balor's mind very hard to read. Humans are easy. Most fae are tough. I can usually only read them if I'm able to touch them. Balor especially. He is a Prince, so that's probably why I have to take extra steps."

I had no idea if she was going to buy my story. If I were her, I probably wouldn't. It sounded like total bullshit. But she didn't know anything about my powers. Plus, she was drunk, and she clearly had power limitations herself. Maybe, just maybe…

"No wonder you weren't able to get anything useful for Balor when he sent you on that mission." She rolled her eyes and slumped against the metal bars. "Your power sucks."

"Gee, thanks."

"Still useful though." She shot me a sharp look. "Don't think you'll get out of it that easily. You're going to read his mind, and you're going to get the information I need. I just need to get you within touching distance so you can read him. Maybe I'll unchain him and drag him over here. He's heavy, but I think I can manage…"

"You could." I shrugged. "Although he could be faking the whole unconscious thing. As soon as you unchain him, he'll be free to retaliate. I know your power is pretty impressive, but this is Balor Beimnech we're talking about. In a fair fight…well, let's just say I'd put money on the Prince. Don't forget what happens when he takes off that eye patch."

She scowled. "I liked you better when you weren't talking shit."

"Not talking shit." I held up my hands in mock surrender. "Just being honest. You know I'm right."

"Yeah. Yeah, I do. Dammit. Here, want another shot?" She passed another overflowing shot glass of whiskey through the bars. I blinked at it, wishing there was some way to avoid getting drunk. But if I refused, she'd know something was up. With a sigh, I poured the liquid down my throat again. This time, it didn't burn quite as much as it had the first time.

Probably because I was now halfway to pissed.

A growl rumbled through the underground station, so deep and so low that I almost thought a train was on its way down the abandoned tracks. Lesley jumped to her feet, her eyes wild with excitement.

"He's woken up," she said. "Time for you to read his mind."

"What is the meaning of this?" Balor asked, his eye so narrow that it was barely more than a slit of red on his face. "Lesley, tell me you aren't the one behind all of this."

"Sorry to disappoint. I've already told the story once tonight, and I don't feel like repeating it," she said. "So, the TLDR of it is basically: you suck, Nemain rules. Your Court is going down so that she can take over. Got it?"

Balor answered with pure, unbridled anger. His entire body thrummed with it. He pulled against his bonds, the chains clanking against the pavement. His hands twisted around the rusted metal, and he yanked with so much strength that time almost seemed to slow. For a moment, I thought he'd managed to actually break free. The floor shook; the metal snapped.

But when the dust settled, he was still trapped.

His eye met mine across the room. So much emotion churned in the red. So much anger. And I couldn't tell if it was directed at her or at me.

He flicked his eye up and down my body, before he shifted his gaze toward where Tiarnan was still slumped in the corner of the cage. "Tell me you're okay, Clark. Tell me she hasn't harmed you."

"Balor, I—"

"Enough of that," Lesley said crisply. "There will be no talking. Only listening."

She shifted back toward the bars and passed a shot glass to me. I hadn't noticed her pouring one. "Drink up. And then I'll take you over to Balor so that you can read his mind."

I eyed the drink warily. "Seriously? I already had two."

"I'm not going to let you out of there until you drink the shot," she said, her voice going hard. "We have to make sure that your powers will be at their best."

If by 'at their best', she meant 'wobbly as hell', then sure. It wasn't that I was a *total* lightweight. I would put my drinking standards more at a medium. Occasionally, I'd enjoy a few. But only a few. And usually spaced out over the course of a couple of hours. She'd given me three straight, full-to-the-brim shots in about ten minutes.

And oh boy, did I feel it. My head felt like it was full of beautiful puffy clouds. I may have even wobbled a bit.

Balor was watching me very carefully as I handed the shot glass back to the sociopathic fae. As my vision blurred a little in the corners, I couldn't help but notice that he looked…fit as fuck. Even tied up in chains. Hell, *because* he was tied up in chains. The way his eye sparked as I drank him in made me want to stride on over there and straddle him.

Ack. Calm yourself, Clark. That's just the booze talking.

Somehow, I was supposed to fight this crazy-ass fae and save the day? How the hell had I gotten myself into this mess?

"Come on." Lesley unlocked the cage, the metal door clanging as she opened it wide. She grabbed my elbow as soon as I finally took a step out of the trap. I breathed in the fresh scent of freedom. Mildew, rat shit, and Jack Daniels.

"Stop stalling." She jerked me forward toward Balor. Whatever pretend friendship we'd formed during our little booze bonding session had flown right out of the proverbial window. Lesley was back in business mode, which meant that I had about a minute, tops, to figure out a real, actual plan that involved a slightly drunk half-fae winning against another really drunk fae who also happened to have the power to stop hearts.

"You're stressing me out," I said in a low voice. "I can't think straight when you have a death grip on my elbow."

"I'll let go when I'm ready to let go."

A moment later, we reached Balor. We both stood over him, staring down at the powerful fae we both called our Prince. How could she even do this to him? My bond squeezed tight between us, pulling my soul closer to his. Even if I'd wanted to, I knew I wouldn't have been able to bring myself to attack him like this. My body wouldn't have let me.

The magic would have stopped it.

"It's going to be hard to read his mind because of the Master bond." The truth, for once. "The magic will stop me from acting against him. I don't understand how it isn't stopping you."

"Ah. Why do you think I'm so drunk?" She grinned. "The booze helps. Trust me. Now, stop stalling. Get down there and read his damn mind. I'm losing patience. Fast."

Finally, she let go of my arm. I knelt down beside Balor and put my trembling hands against his chest. He didn't even flinch when I touched him. Nothing in him changed. He merely continued to stare into my eyes, his soul saying far more than words ever could.

"Okay, I'm ready," I called to Lesley, who stood just behind my shoulder. "What is it that you want me to find out from his thoughts?"

"I need to know who will be named Prince when

Balor's rotting body is found. He'll have something planned. He'll have a successor in place. At first, I thought it would be Duncan, but I know Balor better than that now. That's far too straight-forward. It will be someone else. Someone unexpected."

With a deep breath, I closed my eyes and pushed into Balor's mind. For once, the walls between us were gone. All of the protection he kept built around his thoughts had been extinguished. Instead, he welcomed me. He pulled me closer, inviting me into the very depths of his mind.

Balor? I had no idea if he could hear me. I'd never tried this before. Only Fionn had ever been able to speak to me through his thoughts, and I was terrified that all of my drunken manoeuvrings would end up yielding nothing more than a big fat zero.

I'm here, Clark. Are you okay? Has she hurt you?

Relief punched me in the gut. *Not as much as she's hurt Tiarnan. He's dying. And so is Ondine. Listen, Balor. Lesley plans to kill us all in some crazy attempt to destroy the Court. She's going to make it look like we all murdered each other. She's drunk and half crazy, and she can stop my heart with a single touch. What the hell do I do?*

"Hurry it up," I heard Lesley snap, in actual reality instead of in my head.

"Sorry," I replied. "Like I said, he's hard to read. Almost there…"

You're panicking. Take a deep breath. Calm down. And then remember what I've taught you to do.

What he'd taught me to do?!

But that was just it. I'd only been at his Court for a week. We'd started training, but we hadn't gotten very far. Not after all our arguments. Moira had showed me some pointers with the sword, but I didn't have a goddamn sword. All I had was me.

You're not listening to me. Calm down, Clark.

His voice was soft. Gone was the cold, hard Prince who pushed me away. This was the Balor he rarely let anyone see. The one whose gaze pulled me in, the one whose soul answered to mine. I stared into the very depths of him, and I saw a kind of faith and trust I knew I didn't deserve.

He was the Prince. I was the Courtless half-fae with a past that would make him hate me. And yet, he was putting his very life in my hands. He trusted me to save him.

Slowly, I stood and turned to face my enemy. She cocked her head, flicking her gaze up and down my body as if she were suddenly seeing me as who I was for the very first time. A challenge. An actual opponent. A fae who was going to try to kick her ass.

"What's going on? Did you find out the answer?"

"Yes. I did." With a deep breath, I threw my body into the motion Balor had drilled into my head. I dropped low to the ground and swung my legs in a wide circle. They made contact, knocking Lesley off her feet. She fell hard on the ground, a loud smack echoing through the tunnel.

"Yes, Clark!" Balor shouted.

His encouragement shot another burst of adrenaline through my veins, driving away the booze that threatened to slow my speed. I jumped to my feet, bouncing on the balls of them. But Lesley was a hell of a lot more agile than I'd expected. In an instant, she was back on her feet. And she looked seriously pissed off.

"How dare you." Golden magic sparked around her fingers, and her hand shot out to grab my arm.

She was trying to stop my heart.

I moved without thinking, as if something deep and primal inside of me sparked to life. Slowly, I shifted to the right and watched her hand shoot past my head. Then, I wrapped my fingers around her wrist, twisted her hand away from my face, and slammed it right against her neck.

Her glowing fingers touched her own skin; her eyes went white.

And, this time, it wasn't me who fell into the dark.

30

"Clark Cavanaugh." Ondine shot me a weak smile from her healing ward bed. The nurses had finally let me in to see her. It had been three days, and she was finally strong enough to face the world. Lesley had done a number on her heart, just like she'd done to Tiarnan. But she'd pulled through. They both had. And now Tiarnan was on his way back to his House.

After I'd used Lesley's own powers against her, I'd unlocked Balor's chains just in time for Lesley's heart to restart. She'd been super pissed off, but Balor? There wasn't a word in the English dictionary that fully illustrated how angry he'd been.

The fight had been over within seconds. Balor had won, of course. And strangely, he'd let her live. She was now rotting in a jail cell, waiting for her trial. Word on the street was that she'd end up being ruled a traitor to Faerie. Regardless of what she did, it made me shudder when I thought about her fate. She would be stripped of her power, and then fed to the Sluagh.

As for Nemain, the leader of the Silver Court who had given Lesley her order? No one knew what would happen with that. What she had done was treason against Faerie, but nothing had changed. She still sat on her throne. For now.

I eased into the armchair by Ondine's bed and passed her a bar of chocolate. "Here. Thought you could use some sugary goodness."

"Thanks." She broke off a piece, popped it into her mouth. "Balor told me what you did. I have to admit, I'm shocked you stuck around. I would have thought you'd run from the Court the first chance you got."

"I wasn't going to leave until I found you," I said with a slight smile.

"And so you found me." She raised her eyebrows. "What are you going to do now? You know I won't tell."

I let out a long, slow breath. To be honest? I didn't have a clue. It had been three days since the showdown in the underground, and I'd had more than a dozen chances to get out of here. For some crazy reason, I still hadn't left. And I didn't know when I would.

I didn't know what was stopping me.

Oh wait, yes I did.

"Clark," Balor said in the deep, toe-curling voice of his. He edged into the room, glanced down at me. "I thought I might find you here. Do you have a minute? There's something I want to show you."

"Sure?" Ondine shot me a curious glance that I strategically ignored. "Get some rest. I'll be back later."

I followed Balor out into the corridor, half-afraid that he was going to tell me that Lesley had somehow escaped. But instead, he silently led me out of the healing ward and back into the main halls of the Court. When he finally came to a stop, he pushed open a door that was only a few rooms down from mine. Inside, there was a small desk and an ergonomic chair.

Plus, a laptop, a microphone, and some noise-cancelling headphones. Pretty fancy ones, too.

I turned to Balor, eyebrows arched. "What's this?"

"This," he said in a low murmur. "Is your new podcasting home."

"Wait, what?" My heart lurched in my chest as I stared up at him. His lips curled into a smile, one that would make any warm-blooded woman's insides melt. Including mine. Not that I could give in to those feelings. Despite the moment we'd shared in the underground, nothing had changed between us.

He still didn't want to get involved. He still thought we were a mistake.

"I have thought a lot about it, and I see no reason why you shouldn't be allowed to continue your show," he said, his jaw rippling as he spoke. "But there are rules, Clark. You cannot share any secrets about the Court, and you cannot discuss any ongoing cases. If there's something you wish to share on the podcast that you're unsure about, you have to run it by me first. Is that a deal?"

I blinked at him. Was that a deal? Fuck yes, that was a deal.

"Yeah, I think I can agree to that," I said out loud.

"Does that mean you're staying then?"

"What do you mean?" I asked.

"I heard what Ondine said to you. It's something I've wondered about myself. You clearly didn't want to come here when I found you at your flat, and yet you stayed. To find Ondine. Now that you have, you have no reason to stay." He turned to me then, his red eye sparking. "If you truly want to go, Clark, I won't stand in your way. It's your choice."

This was my chance. I could get the hell out of here. No questions asked. He wouldn't even follow me if I did. He was giving me the option, something I never thought I'd have. No one would ever have to know about my past. My secrets would stay safe. My life would no longer be in danger.

As I looked at Balor, I knew there was only one answer I could give. Four little words that would change my life forever. "I think I'll stay."

Something flickered in his eye. Happiness? Disappointment? I couldn't tell. "Then, it's settled. You will remain a member of this House and this Court."

My breath hitched when that deep, dark magic whispered across my skin. It brushed against my cheek, a soft strand of warmth that curled through me. And then it was gone.

"Since you've decided to stay, you'll need to report to the command station immediately. A new report came in, only moments before I found you in Ondine's room. You have another case, Clark. And this one involves the Sluagh."

The Sluagh? Bloody hell.

Thank you for reading *Live Fae or Die Trying*, the first book in The Paranormal PI Files. Curious about Clark's first meeting with Balor? You can grab the prequel story for free by signing up to my reader newsletter.

Dead Fae Walking, the second book in the series, is now available on Amazon.

ABOUT THE AUTHOR

Jenna Wolfhart is a Buffy-wannabe who lives vicariously through the kick-ass heroines in urban fantasy. After completing a PhD in Librarianship, she became a full-time author and now spends her days typing the fantastical stories in her head. When she's not writing, she loves to stargaze, binge Netflix, and drink copious amounts of coffee.

Born and raised in America, Jenna now lives in England with her husband, her dog, and her mischief of rats.

FIND ME ONLINE
Facebook Reader Group
Instagram
YouTube
Twitter

www.jennawolfhart.com
jenna@jennawolfhart.com